Christmas Claws – A Norwegian Forest Cat Café Cozy Mystery – Book 9

by

Jinty James

Christmas Claws – A Norwegian
Forest Cat Café Cozy Mystery – Book 9

by

Jinty James

ISBN:9798565608151

DEDICATION

To my wonderful mother, who loved
reading about Annie and AJ

CHAPTER 1

"You look amazing!" Lauren Crenshaw admired her cousin Zoe's elf costume.

Consisting of a green, red, and white dress, with striped green and red stockings, and a green hat topped off with a white pom pom, she really looked the part. Her brunette pixie bangs peeked out from under the white fur trim of the hat.

"Brrt!" Annie, Lauren's large and fluffy silver-gray Norwegian Forest Cat, agreed. Her green eyes were lively with curiosity as she studied Zoe's outfit.

"Thanks!" Zoe grinned, her brown eyes sparkling. "I can't believe I haven't taken part in the Christmas play before – it's been so much fun! And I get to play head elf!" She twirled around.

They stood backstage at the town hall in Gold Leaf Valley, a small town in Northern California. It was Wednesday evening and they were getting ready for their first dress rehearsal. The opening – and only – night of the play was fast approaching, and their director, playwright, and lead actor, Father Mike, had seemed nervous every time they had rehearsed.

Lauren, Annie, and Zoe ran the Norwegian Forest Cat Café. Annie led the customers to the table she chose for them, while Lauren and Zoe made cappuccinos, lattes, and mochas. Lauren also created delicious cupcakes.

Today, they'd closed a few minutes early so they wouldn't be late for the early evening rehearsal.

"Zoe, are you ready?" The balding priest of the local Episcopalian church stuck his head around the crimson velvet curtain. "Everyone else is here – apart from Mrs. Adley, who's playing Mrs. Claus."

"Yep." Zoe zipped over to the stage.

"Is it okay if we watch from back here?" Lauren asked, glancing down at Annie, who wore her lavender harness. They'd attended the rehearsals before, but now it all seemed much more serious.

"Of course." Father Mike smiled. "But why don't you two sit out front and be our audience? You can tell us if everything looks good." A worried expression crept over his face. "Or not."

"I'm sure everything will be fine," Lauren assured him.

"Brrt," Annie agreed, her silver-gray fur shining in the overhead lighting.

"I hope so." He checked his watch. "We're still waiting for Mrs. Adley – unless she's arrived since I've been back here."

"No, she's not here," Zoe called.

"I guess we'll just have to start without her," Father Mike said.

The sound of an old-fashioned Christmas carol cut through the air. Father Mike looked at Lauren, and Lauren and Annie looked back at him.

"I think you're ringing," Lauren told him.

"Oh, yes – so I am." He searched in the red jacket of his Santa costume. "New phone with a new ringtone. I'm still not used to it."

Lauren decided to give him some privacy, and she and Annie went to sit out front, in the theater seats.

"Can you see me?" Zoe waved from the stage, in front of a painted backdrop featuring the black night sky sprinkled with silver stars. A large, wooden sleigh painted red took up part of the stage.

"Yes." Lauren smiled.

"Brrt!" Annie perched on the purple velvet chair next to Lauren.

The other cast members appeared from backstage: Ed, Lauren's pastry chef, a big burly man with monster rolling pins for arms, and Mrs. Wagner, who was playing an elf.

It was a small cast, and the play had been written by Father Mike a few years ago. When he had asked if he could put up a flyer at the café advertising auditions, Zoe had jumped at the chance to take part.

Lauren – and Annie – looked expectantly at the priest as he walked onto the stage.

"Folks," he began, his face and tone glum, "I'm afraid I have some bad news. Mrs. Adley has pulled out. She's spending Christmas in Vermont with her family and new grandbaby. She said she's sorry to let us down, but the baby arrived early, and she wants to help out her daughter."

There was a small silence.

"That's totally understandable," Zoe spoke.

"Of course it is," Mrs. Wagner agreed crisply. Spectacles perched on her slightly beaky nose, and a green and white elf hat covered her gray, feather cut hair. "Who wouldn't want to assist their family at such a joyous time?"

"Yeah," Ed said, nodding. The bell on his elf hat jingled. Ed was playing a naughty elf, which Lauren thought was the complete opposite of his real self. Although usually a man of few words, he seemed to enjoy taking part in the play. The rest of his costume consisted of a green, red and white jacket and pants, his elf hat the same as Zoe's, just a little bigger and with the addition of a bell.

"I'm glad you're all taking this so well." Father Mike appeared to relax a little. "But I'm afraid we have a little problem. Who can we get to play Mrs. Claus at such late notice?"

"I would do it," Zoe spoke. "But I love being head elf."

"And I think you're an excellent head elf," Father Mike told her earnestly.

"Lauren, do you want to do it?" Zoe turned to look at her sitting in the audience.

"Me?" Lauren's eyes widened and heat hit her cheeks. "No – I don't think I could." She didn't want to let down Father Mike and the others, but she didn't think she could pull something like that off. She wasn't as outgoing as Zoe.

"I'm sorry," Lauren added, feeling guilty.

"That's perfectly all right," Father Mike told her gently. "Who else could we ask?"

"Hmm." Zoe tapped her cheek. "There's Brooke, the local hairdresser, but she told me the other day she was super busy with everyone wanting to get their hair done for their Christmas parties. And Martha, of course. I bet she'd do it, but I don't know if she'd need to have her walker on stage with her." Martha was a senior – and their friend.

Lauren racked her brains. "What about Claire?" she called out.

"Good thinking!" Zoe nodded. "Yes, Claire might be interested, but she'd need someone to babysit her toddler, Molly, unless Molly could come along to rehearsals."

"Ms. Tobin?" Lauren suggested.

There was a small silence.

Ms. Tobin was one of their regular customers. To start with, she had been their prickliest and most demanding one as well, but had mellowed ever since Lauren, Zoe, and Annie had saved her from an internet scam. But sometimes there were still flashes of the old Ms. Tobin.

"That might work," Father Mike said slowly. "But we need someone who can learn their lines quickly, since we're opening in three days."

"Isn't Ms. Tobin helping out at the senior center right now?" Mrs. Wagner commented. "I thought I heard someone mention it when I was there yesterday."

"Oh." Father Mike's expression fell.

"Who else could we get?" Zoe's gaze flickered around the stage.

Lauren was about to take a deep breath and volunteer, however reluctantly, when:

"Brrt!" *Me!* Annie sat up straight in the theater chair.

Zoe's mouth parted. "Of course!" She giggled. "Annie could play Mrs. Claus."

"Brrt!" Annie jumped off the chair and leaped onto the stage, the lead from her harness dangling behind her.

"Annie!" Lauren started after her and climbed onto the stage.

The Norwegian Forest Cat hopped into the sled, her mouth tilted up at the corners, as if she were smiling.

"Brrt!" *I can play Mrs. Claus!*

Father Mike smiled. So did Lauren. And Ed. Mrs. Wagner did so reluctantly.

"That would be a wonderful solution," the priest said, "if it's okay with Lauren." He glanced at her.

Annie looked so pleased with herself that Lauren didn't have the heart to deny her fur baby.

"If it's okay with everyone else," Lauren replied.

"Yes!" Zoe high-fived her. "This is going to be awesome!"

"But will your cat know to sit still in the sled?" Mrs. Wagner asked. "Or is she going to jump out and run around the stage when she's not supposed to?"

"I think Annie will know what to do," Zoe replied before Lauren had a chance. "She's been watching the rehearsals with Lauren."

"And she doesn't run around the café," Lauren replied. "She leads customers to their table, and sits with them if they'd like her to, but if they don't, she relaxes in her basket."

"I think Annie could really draw in the crowds," Father Mike said.

"And it wouldn't be like anything this town has seen before." Ed nodded, the bell on his cap jingling.

"But Annie won't have any lines as she can't talk," Mrs. Wagner pointed out. "How is the dialogue going to work if Mrs. Claus doesn't speak?"

"Brrt!" Annie said.

"I think that's how." Lauren gave Annie a loving look.

"Yes, Annie can say her lines in Norwegian Forest Cat talk." Zoe grinned.

"And I can carry the rest of the dialogue when we're in the sleigh," Father Mike said.

"Well, if you're sure, Father," Mrs. Wagner said doubtfully.

"I think Annie's sure," Lauren said.

"Yep!" Zoe winked.

"Then it's settled." Father Mike beamed at them. "Welcome to the cast, Annie."

"Brrp." *Thank you.* Annie settled down in the sleigh, looking like she never wanted to get out of it.

"What if Annie wears a Christmas hat?" Zoe proposed. "Like the one you're wearing, Father Mike?"

"I don't know if she'd like that." Lauren furrowed her brow, glancing at Annie, who didn't seem concerned at all about the prospect.

"We could try it and see," Father Mike suggested. "And if Annie doesn't like it, she doesn't have to wear it."

"Okay." Lauren nodded.

"We might have a hat small enough backstage," Zoe said.

"We could check after rehearsal," Father Mike replied. "I think we should just get started now, before we run out of time." He glanced at his watch.

"Where do you want this, Father Mike?"

Two men in their early forties appeared from back stage, carrying a large scenery backdrop depicting Santa's workshop, with toys in various stages of production.

"We're not quite ready for that yet, Jay and Kyle," the priest told them. "We're going to start with the scene featuring Santa and Mrs. Claus in the sleigh."

The two brothers had recently moved to the small town and had joined the play as backstage crew. Martha had told Lauren and Zoe that their mother was in assisted living nearby.

"That's a cat." Jay did a double take as he noticed Annie. "In the sled." His eyebrows shot up to his forehead. He was wiry, and of medium height, his hair cut in a fashionable spiky cut, and stubble covering his chin.

"Annie is joining the cast and playing Mrs. Claus," Father Mike told them.

"I've never heard of that before." Kyle, his brother, gave Annie a quizzical glance. He was a little taller than Jay, and his brown hair was cut in a boyish style that suited his clean-shaven look.

"I'll make sure she's okay," Lauren spoke. She was very protective of Annie.

"Me too," Zoe added.

"And me," Ed said gruffly.

"And me, of course," Father Mike told them.

Everyone looked at Mrs. Wagner, including Annie.

"And me too, I suppose." The woman sighed. "Wait until they hear about this at the senior center."

"They'll love it," Zoe assured her. "In fact, with Annie in the play, it should be a sell out!"

"Which would be a very good thing indeed," Father Mike said. "The ticket sales will go toward the local wildlife sanctuary."

"Let's get started then," Mrs. Wagner suggested.

Lauren watched the dress rehearsal, proud of Annie's prowess. She seemed to know exactly when Father Mike paused, waiting for a response from her. Her brrts and brrps seemed to provide the perfect answer to his remarks.

Father Mike finished the scene by saying, "Well, Mrs. Claus, do you think I should enter my workshop now?"

"Brrt," Annie answered, her green eyes shining with delight.

"You're a natural, Annie," Zoe praised.

"Yep." Ed nodded.

"You were wonderful, Annie." Father Mike turned to her, still sitting in the sled with him. "Thank you."

"Brrt!" *It was fun!*

"Now we can start the next scene, which takes place in my – Santa's – workshop," the priest said. "Jay and Kyle, could you change the set now, please?"

"Yes, Father." Kyle gestured to his brother. "Come on."

Lauren watched them wheel away the starry backdrop before putting in place the workshop scenery.

"How's Mrs. Snuggle?" Zoe asked as they waited to resume their rehearsal.

"She hasn't hissed at me for a while now," Father Mike said, his face lighting up. "And last night she even sat in my lap. It was only for a few minutes, though."

The priest had recently adopted a white Persian, who was a former show cat. Her full name was Mrs. Snuggle Face Furry Frost but everyone had developed the habit of calling her Mrs. Snuggle for short.

"I'm sure she'll realize how lucky she is to have you looking after her," Lauren told him. The grumpy feline did not seem to make friends easily – either of the human or animal variety.

"Brrt!" Annie added, still sitting in the sleigh.

"Have you gotten her spayed yet?" Zoe asked.

"Yes, a few weeks ago," he answered. "And now I'm putting together a little Christmas stocking for her. Just so she knows someone loves her."

"Ohhh." Lauren misted up. Father Mike lived alone, but she hadn't realized he'd been lonely until he'd admitted it when Mrs. Snuggle had come into his life. He always seemed so busy, helping his congregation and raising funds for good causes, that she hadn't thought he would have time to be lonesome. She just hoped Mrs. Snuggle appreciated his kindness.

"Annie's getting one too." Zoe lowered her voice.

"So is AJ." Ed spoke. Annie had discovered AJ as a stray Maine Coon kitten in the garden, and had brought her into the café kitchen. Ed had instantly fallen in love with the little brown tabby, and it seemed to be mutual.

"I hope Santa Claus won't forget us," Zoe joked.

"I don't think so," Lauren answered. She'd already bought her cousin's gift and had hidden it in her closet. All she had to do was wrap it.

"Perhaps we should get started," Mrs. Wagner suggested. "I do have to get home tonight."

"Of course." Father Mike nodded. "Let's take our places and start the scene."

"Annie, you're not in this part of the play." Lauren scooped up the cat and cuddled her.

"Brrp." Annie's lower lip jutted out.

"We can sit in the audience," Lauren whispered to her.

Annie seemed mollified as Lauren carried her to one of the plush theater chairs. "We can watch Zoe and Ed. And Father Mike, of course," she murmured.

Annie sat up straight as Father Mike, in his role of Santa, entered the workshop and asked for the toys for all the good boys and girls.

Zoe played the head elf in charge of the gifts and making sure everything was on schedule, bossing around Mrs. Wagner and Ed. It turned out that the toy making was *not* on schedule as Ed's character was stealing some of the toys to keep for himself. The scene ended with Zoe chasing Ed around the stage, with Mrs. Wagner jumping up and down – or as well as she could – from the sidelines.

Lauren thought Ed was a good sport for taking on the role, but he'd told her gruffly a few weeks ago that he'd wanted to help out Father Mike who was always doing good for other people.

"That was wonderful, everyone." Father Mike beamed. "Now, we have the final scene, where Mrs. Claus – Annie –

and I hop in the sleigh and deliver the presents to all the girls and boys."

"Brrt!" Annie jumped down from her chair and bounded up to the stage. Lauren followed.

"That's right, Annie," the priest told her. "We'll sit in the sleigh just like we did before, and say our lines."

"Brrp." *Okay.*

Father Mike clambered into the sleigh.

"Now it's time to deliver the gifts to all the good boys and girls, Mrs. Claus. And then we'll go home, feed the reindeer, and have a hot drink to celebrate our night's work."

"Brrt," Annie said in approval. "Brrt!"

Everyone laughed and gave Annie and Father Mike a round of applause. Annie lapped up the attention, looking very pleased with herself.

"Maybe this will work after all," Mrs. Wagner remarked.

"Thank you, everyone," Father Mike spoke. "Now, if we could meet again tomorrow at the same time for another dress rehearsal. Lauren, is that okay with you and Annie?"

Lauren looked at Annie, who answered.

"Brrt." *Yes.*

"Yes, Father," Lauren replied.

"See you at seven p.m." Father Mike smiled.

"I can't wait until I tell Chris that Annie's in the play," Zoe said as Lauren and Annie followed her to the dressing room. "He was going to be here tonight and help with the scenery, but he was asked to work an extra shift." She made a face.

Chris was Zoe's boyfriend, and a paramedic. He'd recently transferred from Sacramento to Gold Leaf Valley, and Zoe was thrilled. So was Lauren. She thought Zoe and Chris were perfect for each other.

"I don't know if Mitch will believe it," Lauren said as Zoe shimmied out of her elf costume and into her jeans and red sweater.

She'd been dating Mitch for over a year now and it was getting very serious. They'd met each other's parents and they spoke to each other practically every night on the phone, as well as seeing each

18

other a few times per week, unless Mitch's work as a police detective forced him to work overtime.

"He might," Zoe said thoughtfully. "After all, Annie did call him on the phone when we were in danger."

"That's true."

"We should find a hat for Annie." Zoe turned to the feline. "Would you like that?"

"Brrt!" *Yes!*

"There's a chest over here containing accessories for the costumes." Zoe hurried over to the corner and opened a big wooden box. "Let's see." She rifled through the contents, pulling out feather boas, scarves, and mittens.

"Don't you need to be careful with all that?" Lauren was half amused and half shocked.

"This is all old stuff, mostly from thrift stores." Zoe's voice was muffled from the depths of the chest. "Oh, look!" She straightened and dangled a red Santa hat with white trim. "It might be small enough to fit Annie."

Lauren took it from her, the velvet soft against her fingers. "It looks like it was made for a small child – or a baby."

"Or a cat." Zoe grinned.

"Brrp?" Annie nosed the hat.

"Do you want to try it on?" Lauren asked her. "It goes on your head."

"Brrt!" Annie wriggled her head under the cap, as if attempting to put it on herself.

"Here." Lauren gently placed it on Annie's head.

"You look great, Annie." Zoe grinned. "It's just the right size for you. Take a look in the mirror." She pointed to a long mirror on the rear of the dressing room door.

"Brrt!" *I look pretty!* Annie peered at her reflection, her green eyes shining with pleasure.

The white trim of the hat sat above her eyes, and didn't seem too tight – or too loose.

"I think it's perfect." Lauren smiled at Annie. "But let me know if you want to take it off anytime, or it starts annoying you."

"Brrt." *I will.*

"I guess we should go home now." Zoe sighed.

"Yes. We have to get up early tomorrow to open the café." Lauren glanced at her practical white wristwatch.

"At least opening night will be on Saturday and we can sleep late on Sunday."

"Definitely." Lauren nodded. Rehearsals had been running for a few weeks now, and she and Annie had accompanied Zoe, mainly for moral support, although Lauren had helped out backstage when needed.

They left the dressing room. Just as they were about to exit through the stage door, they heard voices.

"You'd better pay up, young man." It was Mrs. Wagner speaking harshly. "I know what you did. And I won't let you get away with it."

"It was an accident." It sounded like Jay. "And I said I'd pay you. I've just been busy."

"I'll make sure he does pay you." Kyle, Jay's brother, spoke. "I'm sorry, Mrs. Wagner."

"Make sure you do." Mrs. Wagner sounded a little mollified. "I have enough to deal with at my age without chasing you two for money."

The sound of footsteps alerted them that the trio had moved away.

"They must have been just outside the stage door," Zoe commented.

"Maybe we should wait a second, and make sure the coast is clear," Lauren suggested.

"Brrt," Annie agreed.

After a couple of minutes, Zoe peeked around the old wooden door.

"I can't see anyone," she stage-whispered.

"Good," Lauren whispered back.

"Let's go!"

They trooped out the door and walked to Lauren's white car, the street lamp shining down on it. Although it was only nine p.m., the sky was velvety black with the occasional twinkling star.

"I wonder what that was all about," Zoe mused.

"I hope it wasn't anything serious." Lauren frowned as she opened the rear door for Annie. The cat hopped into her carrier, and Lauren fastened it.

"Why do they owe Mrs. Wagner money?" Zoe persisted.

"Why don't you ask her?" Lauren teased.

"I will, the next time I see her."

"Zoe!"

"She might need our help," Zoe said in all seriousness. "After all, we have solved several murders."

"Mm." In Lauren's mind, they'd snooped where perhaps they shouldn't have, but she had to admit that Zoe was correct in a way. They'd helped flush out the killer more than once.

They arrived home a few minutes later. Lauren had left the porch lamp on, and the light in the living room. She'd inherited the small Victorian cottage, along with the café next door, from her Gramms.

After giving Annie her supper – chicken in gravy – she checked her messages. One from Mitch, asking how the first dress rehearsal had gone. She told Zoe.

"Wait until he hears about Annie becoming the star of the show." She giggled. Then sobered. "If you ever get to see him. Since Chris moved in, they've been hanging out together."

"I know," Lauren replied ruefully. There weren't many rentals available in the small town, so Chris was staying with Mitch on a temporary basis. Which meant that sometimes it seemed the two friends spent more time doing guy stuff together than they spent with Lauren and Zoe.

Not that Lauren minded, she told herself. She was glad the two guys enjoyed being roomies. She just wished she was seeing Mitch a little more often right now.

But even if Chris hadn't moved in with his buddy, would she actually be seeing more of Mitch? With attending the rehearsals, and Mitch's work, there wouldn't be many opportunities for them to get together in the evenings. Hopefully he'd be able to stop by the café tomorrow.

"Chris promised me he'd be there on opening night. I hope so."

"I'm sure he will," Lauren assured her.

"Brrt!" Annie had finished her supper and joined them in the living room.

"Thanks, Annie." Zoe smiled at her. "I guess we'd better go to bed if we want to open the café on time tomorrow."

Getting up early was the only drawback to running a café that Lauren could think of.

"Yes." She yawned.

CHAPTER 2

The next morning, Lauren crunched granola while Zoe munched whole wheat toast slathered with butter. Annie had already eaten her beef and liver.

"I wonder if Father Mike has thought to put up new posters for the play." Zoe's brown eyes sparkled. "We'll need them, so everyone knows Annie is playing Mrs. Claus."

"Great idea." Lauren glanced at Annie, who sat next to her at the kitchen table. "What do you think?"

"Brrt!"

"I can make them during our quiet periods today," Zoe said.

"If we have any."

Business had been very good the last couple of weeks. The weather had turned chilly, and Lauren wondered if it might even snow. She would love to experience a white Christmas, even if it was only for one day – or half a day.

"I think I should make an extra batch of cupcakes today." Her sweet treats had been selling out every day lately, along with Ed's feather light Danishes.

"Ooh – are you making your new gingerbread cupcakes?" Zoe's eyes lit up.

"Yes." Gingerbread cakes with ginger flavored frosting and a red and white striped miniature candy cane had proved to be a big hit with their customers.

Mitch had suggested a super vanilla cupcake a couple of months ago, and she was still working on that request. Since it was for him, she wanted it to be super special.

"Make sure you put one away for me."

"I will." No wonder she had curves – her new creation had her reaching for one more often than she should.

They walked through the private hallway connecting the cottage to the café and started setting up.

The interior walls were pale yellow, and the furniture consisted of pine tables and chairs – right now, the chairs were stacked on the tables. A string-art picture of a cupcake with lots of pink frosting decorated one of the walls – evidence of one of Zoe's past hobbies.

And of course, Annie's pink cat bed on a low shelf, where she could relax when she wasn't seating customers.

Faint notes of hazelnut and cocoa scented the air. As well as lattes and cappuccinos, they made regular and dark hot chocolate, as well as tea, such as Earl Grey, for their customers. Cupcakes, Danishes, and an array of Paninis rounded out their offerings along with a refrigerator full of chilled juices, and water.

Lauren unlocked the oak and glass door right on the dot of nine-thirty.

"I'll start making the posters now." Zoe pulled out a drawer behind the counter and grabbed a white sheet of paper and a black marker.

After a couple of minutes, Zoe held up her work.

Come and see Annie starring as Mrs. Claus in the Christmas Play!
7p.m. Saturday Night at the Town Hall.

"It looks good." Lauren admired it. "And you've drawn Annie's portrait on it."

"She's easy to draw," Zoe said modestly. In the last few months, she'd embarked on pottery as her new hobby and had made mugs featuring Annie in different poses. She'd sketched Annie's picture herself, and Lauren had to admit her cousin had a talent for art. The customers loved the mugs and it was good advertising for the café as well.

"Look, Annie." Zoe held up the poster so Annie could see it from her basket.

"Brrt!" Annie sat up straight as she studied it.

"Will Father Mike be okay with this?" Lauren asked. She was proud that Annie was in the play, but she didn't want to step on any toes – or should that be paws?

"Because I've called Annie the star of the show?"

"Mm-hm."

"I'm sure he won't mind," Zoe said. "But I'll call and check with him."

"Good idea."

"He said it sounds great." Zoe shoved her phone back in her jeans' pocket. "And I should make as many as I want."

"Let's put this in the window."

After they placed it prominently in the big window facing the street, they smiled at each other.

"Now all we need are some customers," Zoe declared.

"Brrt!"

A few minutes later, Mrs. Wagner walked into the café, looking warm in her winter outfit of a periwinkle quilted jacket and matching pants.

"Hi, Mrs. Wagner." Zoe pounced on her. "What can we get you?"

"Give me a minute to study your offerings, Zoe," she replied.

Their usual rule was that customers came to the counter to order, and Lauren and Zoe brought out their treats. But they relaxed this rule for the elderly, infirm, and harried. Since Mrs. Wagner was really neither, although she did appear to be around sixty-five, Lauren surmised that Zoe wanted to grill her for information – specifically, what they had overheard last night when leaving the theater.

Mrs. Wagner perused the contents of the glass case – Lauren's new gingerbread creation, as well as triple chocolate ganache, and blueberry crumble cupcakes.

"You don't have Ed's honeyed walnut Danish?" Mrs. Wagner asked, her mouth pursed.

"It's in the oven right now," Lauren said. "It might be ready in thirty minutes or so."

"I don't have time to wait." She sighed. "I'll have a gingerbread cupcake. They are quite good."

"Thank you," Lauren replied.

"Would you like something to drink?" Zoe asked. "Latte, cappuccino, mocha, hot chocolate, tea?"

"Just a regular latte, thank you," Mrs. Wagner replied.

Usually Annie trotted over to a customer as soon as they entered the shop, but today she seemed to realize that Mrs. Wagner hadn't been ready to be seated. Now, however, the feline came over to her.

"Brrt?" she asked enquiringly.

"I'm ready to sit down now, Annie," Mrs. Wagner replied, her expression lightening a little.

"Brrt." *This way.* Annie led the senior to a small table near the counter.

"We'll be right over with your order," Lauren promised.

Annie ambled back to her basket. Apparently, Mrs. Wagner didn't seem in the mood to chat with her.

"I'll take the cupcake over," Zoe whispered. She plopped the treat onto a white plate and zoomed over to their customer.

"These are delicious," she enthused to Mrs. Wagner. "Lauren is making your latte."

"Thank you." Mrs. Wagner nodded.

Zoe leaned in. "How come Jay and Kyle owe you money?"

"What?" Mrs. Wagner frowned. "How on earth do you know that?"

"We couldn't help overhearing last night at the theater," Zoe told her.

"We weren't eavesdropping," Lauren said, as she walked over with the coffee. She'd added a peacock design to the top of the micro foam. The advanced latte art course they'd taken in Sacramento a while ago had really paid off.

"Yeah, we were just about to leave when we heard you tell them, *'I know what you did.'*" Zoe's expression was keen with curiosity. "What did they do?"

Sometimes Lauren wished her cousin wasn't so impulsive, but she had to admit she'd like to know as well. Although …

"It's not really any of our business," she reminded her cousin.

"No, it's not," Mrs. Wagner told her. She stabbed her fork into the cupcake, the cheery red and white candy cane falling to the side of the plate with a clatter. "But I'll tell you, anyway. They've recently moved in next door to me, and the first thing they did – well, Jay did – was to remove part of the wooden fence between our properties and in doing so, dug up my very rare and valuable rosebush."

"Why would they do that?" Zoe scrunched her nose.

"Because they think they can do anything they like." Mrs. Wagner sipped her coffee, not seeming to notice the latte art.

"Jay gave me some lame excuse about wanting to plant hops. Apparently, he wants to make his own beer." She tsked. "Kyle is okay, I suppose, but I do not like Jay. He thinks if he does something wrong, someone else will bail him out. And life isn't like that."

"No," Lauren replied.

"Not all the time," Zoe agreed. "Is that why they owe you money?" she persisted.

"Yes." Mrs. Wagner nodded vigorously. "I told them it was a very rare rose and it had cost me a lot of money to buy it a few years ago – two hundred dollars, would you believe – but I'd saved up for it and it produces the most amazing flowers you've ever seen. And the perfume!" Mrs. Wagner closed her eyes as if remembering the scent. "I'd never experienced anything like it. And now they've destroyed it. And it's not as if I can just go out and buy another. I've called nurseries everywhere, and most of them have never heard of it. And the employees who know what I'm talking about said they can't get their hands on it."

"You can't replant it and see if it will grow again?" Lauren asked. Although she had a backyard and a small front garden, she didn't have much experience in growing things, apart from her tiny herb garden at the rear of the café.

"I tried that," Mrs. Wagner said mournfully. "It just died."

"Oh." Lauren didn't know what to say.

"I don't blame you for wanting Jay to pay for the damage," Zoe said indignantly.

"Thank you." Mrs. Wagner nodded. "Whenever I press him about it, he keeps saying he'll pay tomorrow, or next week, but it's been three weeks now, and he still hasn't coughed up."

"What about hiring a lawyer?" Zoe asked.

"That will probably cost more money than the rose bush was worth. And I just don't have the spare cash to do something like that." Mrs. Wagner sighed. "The only thing I can think of is to keep asking him for payment every time I see him."

"Perhaps Father Mike could talk to him," Lauren suggested.

"Oh, I don't want to bother the poor man," Mrs. Wagner said. "He's so busy, running here and there, looking after his congregation. And now he's taken in that Persian show cat." She tsked. "I took over some cookies I'd baked, since he does so much for everyone, and the cat hissed at me. Can you believe that?"

Unfortunately, Lauren could. Mrs. Wagner looked like an indignant hawk in that moment, and Mrs. Snuggle did not seem to like any humans at the best of times – apart from Father Mike, possibly.

They left Mrs. Wagner to enjoy her order.

"Wow," Zoe muttered as they headed toward the counter. "No wonder she sounded cranky last night when we overheard their conversation."

"No wonder," Lauren echoed. She just hoped Mrs. Wagner's problem would be solved to her satisfaction.

Martha barreled into the café, Annie running to greet her.

"Brrt!" She hopped onto the seat of her friend's walker without waiting for an invitation.

"Hi, cutie pie!" The gray-haired woman winked at Annie. "Where should I sit?"

"Brrt!" *This way!* Annie directed her with a series of brrts and brrps until they stopped at a four-seater table in the middle of the room.

"Hi, girls." Martha waved to Lauren and Zoe once she sat down. "Is it true Annie is going to star in the play?"

"Brrt!" *Yes!* Annie jumped on the pine chair next to Martha's.

"Yes," Mrs. Wagner replied from her table.

"Yes," Lauren and Zoe chorused.

They hurried over to Martha – and Annie.

"You must tell me all about it." Martha grinned. Although she needed her walker to get around, she was full of energy.

"We will," Zoe promised. "Did you see my poster in the window?"

"Yes." Martha nodded, her short curls springing around her head. "Good stuff. But I also heard it down at the senior center this morning."

"Don't look at me," Mrs. Wagner said from her table. "I haven't told anyone yet."

"That place is a hotbed of gossip," Lauren mused.

"You bet!" Martha winked.

"What can we get you?" Zoe asked.

Martha ordered her usual hot chocolate crammed with marshmallows.

"I've already bought a ticket for the play, even before I knew you were going to be in it, Annie." She turned to the cat. "Now I'm glad I did. I don't want to miss out."

"Brrp." *Thank you.* Annie nudged Martha's arm.

"It's going to be amazing," Zoe enthused. "And you'll get to see me play the head elf." She struck a pose.

Lauren observed it was the same pose as last night and smiled to herself.

"I can't wait!"

They gave Martha her order and left her to enjoy her time with Annie.

"I hope Mrs. Finch has bought a ticket," Zoe fretted. "I don't want her to miss out on seeing Annie – and me – in the play."

"I'm sure she has," Lauren assured her. "And if she hasn't, we could buy one for her."

"As a Christmas present!" Zoe brightened. "That's a great idea."

"We can ask her when she comes in today," Lauren proposed.

"Especially since we won't be going to her house for craft club tomorrow night."

Craft club – a Zoe invention – took place Friday nights at Mrs. Finch's. It had previously been called knitting/crochet/string-art/beading/pottery club, evidence of Zoe's hobbies, until they'd finally decided to just call it craft club. They'd both started with knitting which Lauren had stuck with, but Zoe had ventured out into the world of handcrafts until she finally seemed to have settled on pottery – for now, anyway.

But with the play on Saturday night, and the final dress rehearsal Friday, they'd had to regretfully cancel their craft club evening, as there were only four members, including Annie.

"I'm sure Ms. Tobin will buy a ticket when she knows Annie will be in the play," Zoe said.

"I think you're right." Lauren nodded.

"And Claire and little Molly."

Just as Zoe mentioned their names, the mother-daughter duo entered the café.

"Annie!" Molly waved her chubby arms as her tall, athletic mother pushed her in the stroller.

"Brrt!" Annie jumped down from the chair and ran to greet her friend.

"I think she's getting too old to be pushed around," Claire confided to them as Molly gently patted Annie. "But I don't think she can walk here all the way from our house."

"Why don't you two sit here with me?" Martha suggested. "Then Annie can sit with all of us."

"Yeah!" Molly beamed, her blonde curls bouncing around her face.

"Thank you." Claire smiled at Martha.

"Cino, cino," Molly chanted, referring to her usual order of a babycino. Made of frothy steamed milk, with pink and white marshmallows and a sprinkle of chocolate powder, it was a treat the toddler enjoyed immensely.

Claire ordered her usual latte, and a gingerbread cupcake. "You can share mine, darling," she told Molly.

"Yeah!" Molly clapped her hands.

Lauren smiled to herself, wondering what the toddler's reaction would be when they told her Annie would be playing Mrs. Claus in the play.

Martha beat them to it.

"Are you two going to the Christmas show on Saturday night?" she asked. "I am. And guess who will be in it?"

"Zoe!" Molly pointed to her. "Elf!"

"That's right." Martha nodded. "And Annie is going to be in it."

Molly's mouth fell open as she stared at the cat and then back at Martha.

"Really?" Claire asked.

"Yes," Lauren replied.

"Brrt!"

"As Mrs. Claus!" Zoe told them.

"Ooooooh!!!!!!!" Molly's expression was full of admiration as she gazed at Annie.

"Just as well I'd already bought tickets," Claire said wryly. "Because I wouldn't get any peace until I did."

"And there's a good chance it will be a sell out because Annie's in it." Zoe grinned.

They headed to the counter to fill the orders.

"If we tell every customer that Annie is going to be in the play, I bet Father Mike sells the remainder of the tickets today," Zoe commented.

"I hope so," Lauren replied. The local wildlife sanctuary was a worthy cause, and Father Mike could raise a lot of money.

The morning passed quickly.

When Hans entered the café, Annie ran to greet him. The dapper German in his sixties was one of her favorite people.

"Brrt!"

"Where shall I sit, hmm, *Liebchen?*" A dapper man in his sixties, his faded blue eyes twinkled down at her.

"Brrt!" *With me!* Annie led him slowly to a two-seater table near the counter.

"Hi, Hans!" Zoe greeted him as she leaned over the counter.

"Hello, Zoe, and Lauren."

"Hi." Lauren smiled as she finished the latte art on a cappuccino. This time it was a tulip.

"I have heard all about Annie." Hans beamed at the Norwegian Forest Cat sitting next to him. "You are to be the star of the show, *Liebchen*!"

"Brrt!"

Zoe took his order, and they both chatted to him when they brought over his cappuccino and gingerbread cupcake.

"I have already bought my ticket," Hans told them. "Now I am glad I did. I do not want to miss out on seeing you, Annie."

"I thought I could record the play on my phone so AJ, and Annie's friend Toby, could watch it later," Lauren said.

"That's a great idea!" Zoe grinned. "I'm sure Father Mike won't mind."

They left Hans to enjoy his visit with Annie.

"We could have an early dinner before rehearsals tonight," Zoe said as they headed back to the counter.

"Definitely," Lauren said. She didn't know if she could wait until nine p.m. or even later.

"Let's get pizza."

"Okay." It was one of their favorite meals, although Lauren tried to ensure she ate plenty of vegetables – most of the time – as well.

"I'll order it after we close this afternoon and clean up."

Lauren nodded, her attention focused on the person walking through the door.

"Hi, Ms. Tobin," she greeted one of their regulars.

"Hi!" Zoe waved to her.

"Brrt?" Annie looked up from her conversation with Hans. With a murmured, "Brrp," she hopped down from her chair and trotted to greet the fifty-something woman.

Ms. Tobin wore a fawn sweater with matching skirt, just right for the chilly December weather. The color combination complimented her brown hair.

"Hello, dear." Ms. Tobin smiled down at Annie.

"Brrt." *Hello.*

Annie led her to a table near the counter.

"What I should get today, Annie?" Lauren heard her faintly.

Annie placed her paw on the laminated menu that was on the table.

"Yes, I think you're right." Ms. Tobin nodded. "A cupcake sounds perfect."

She rose and walked toward the counter. Annie ran back to Hans while Ms. Tobin ordered.

"I understand, *Liebchen*," Hans told her. "You are in demand today."

"Brrp." Annie bunted his arm.

"I shall see you in the play on Saturday night."

"Brrt!" *Yes!*

Lauren turned her attention to Ms. Tobin.

"I'll have a large latte and one of your cupcakes, Lauren. Let me see." She perused the offerings in the glass case. "Yes, I'll try your new gingerbread creation."

"It won't be long," Lauren promised.

"Ready in a jiffy," Zoe added cheerfully.

"I bought a ticket to the play this morning," Ms. Tobin told them. "I heard at the senior center that Annie will be playing Mrs. Claus."

"Yes, it's true." Lauren nodded as she steamed milk. She explained about Mrs. Adley dropping out of the play.

"She's been waiting a long time for her first grandchild," Ms. Tobin remarked. "I can see why she would rather spend Christmas with her family." She looked a little wistful.

Ms. Tobin returned to her table. Annie said goodbye to Hans and joined her.

"Do you think Ms. Tobin has any family?" Zoe plated the cupcake.

"I don't know." Ms. Tobin was quite a private person.

Zoe took the treat over to the table.

"Thank you." Ms. Tobin smiled briefly. "Annie has been keeping me company." She turned to Annie. "I think you will be excellent in the play, dear."

"Brrt." *Thank you.*

They left Ms. Tobin to enjoy her time with Annie.

"I must be going now." Hans approached the counter to pay his bill. He clinked some coins into the tip jar.

"Thanks." Zoe smiled.

Zoe and Ed shared the tips. Since Lauren owned the café, she didn't think it fair to take a cut of the tips as well.

"I shall see you at the theater on Saturday." Hans beamed.

They waved goodbye to him.

"Total sell out." Zoe nodded. "Everyone is going to be at the town hall to see the play."

"I think you're right."

Lauren's attention was snagged by the tall, lean, and muscular man who strode into the shop. In his early thirties, he wore a blue button-down shirt and charcoal slacks.

Mitch Denman.

"Hi," he greeted her.

"Hi," Lauren replied softly. Every time she saw him, her heart beat faster, even though they'd been dating for over a year.

"Where's Chris?" Zoe glanced behind him, as if expecting her boyfriend to suddenly appear.

"He's working a shift."

"Again?" Zoe frowned.

"Since he's new down here, he doesn't want to rock the boat. Not yet, anyway," Mitch explained. "But he said to tell you he'll be at the theater tomorrow night to help backstage."

"Good." Zoe's expression brightened.

"I'm sorry we haven't seen much of each other lately," he murmured to Lauren. "Between work and Chris crashing at my place …"

"I understand," Lauren replied. She noticed Zoe had moved to the other end of the counter, but wondered if her cousin could still overhear them.

"Detective Castern has gone home for the holidays," Mitch continued. "So I've been doing some overtime. I haven't been hanging out with Chris every night."

"I didn't think you were," Lauren said. She'd been a little disappointed that she hadn't seen Mitch as often as usual recently, but she was glad that he had a good friend to spend time with, like she had in Zoe – and Annie.

"I'll make it up to you," he promised. "What about tonight – or tomorrow

48

night?" He looked rueful. "Tomorrow's craft club – or is it dress rehearsal?"

"Tonight is dress rehearsal too," Lauren said regretfully. "And since Annie is playing Mrs. Claus, I need to be there."

He blinked. "She's what?"

"You mean you haven't heard?" Zoe jumped into the conversation from the other end of the counter. "I think you're the only person in here today who didn't know!"

Lauren quickly told him what had transpired last night.

"I was coming to watch the play with you anyway, but I definitely have to see this." He smiled, glancing around the café. "Where's Annie now?"

"Over there." She gestured to the small table, where the feline appeared to be listening to Ms. Tobin.

"Tell her congratulations from me." His dark brown eyes were warm as he returned his attention to Lauren.

"I will."

"What about Sunday?" he asked. "I could come over and we could have lunch. I'll organize it."

"I'd like that." She smiled.

His phone buzzed a few minutes later, and he left with a latte and a gingerbread cupcake, promising to call her that night.

"Maybe Chris and I can do something on Sunday," Zoe mused as soon as Mitch left the café, "Since you'll be occupied." She winked.

"I hope so." Lauren felt her cheeks heat a little. Would she always have that reaction to her cousin speaking about Mitch?

"I love that Chris transferred down here," Zoe continued. "And it's cool that he's roomies with Mitch. I mean, we're roomies – with Annie, of course." She glanced over at Annie keeping Ms. Tobin company. "But it would be nice if Chris stopped by the café sometimes. Like he did when he lived in Sacramento."

Before Lauren could open her mouth to say something, Zoe continued, "Yes, I know he's the new guy at work, like Mitch reminded me. It's just – I don't know." She sighed.

Her sudden bout of uncertainty wasn't like the sunny, impulsive cousin Lauren knew. But Zoe had experienced some disastrous internet dates before meeting Chris – in real life. And their romance had progressed slowly at first – perhaps even more slowly than Lauren and Mitch's.

"Tell him how you feel." Lauren touched her shoulder. "Maybe he's feeling the same way."

"You think?" Zoe brightened.

In Lauren's opinion, they were the perfect couple. Chris's laidback, easy going nature complemented Zoe's live wire personality.

"Yes."

CHAPTER 3

"Hi, Mrs. Finch," Zoe called out that afternoon.

Their friend, and one of their favorite customers, tapped her way into the café with her walking stick. Her gray hair was piled on top of her head in a bun, and she wore glasses. She looked warmly dressed in a large coat and beige skirt, with thick stockings in a tan shade.

"Brrt!" Annie ran to greet her.

"Hello, dear." Mrs. Finch beamed down at the big fluffy cat, the orange rouge on her cheeks blooming like California poppies. "Where should I sit?"

"Brrt!" *Over here!*

Annie slowly led her to a four-seater near the counter. The lunch rush was over and there were only a few customers seated at various tables.

"What can we get you?" Lauren hurried over.

"I think I'll have a latte and one of your cupcakes, Lauren, dear." Mrs. Finch sank into the pine chair.

"Are you okay?" Zoe zoomed over to join them.

"I'm perfectly fine." Mrs. Finch waved a wobbly hand in the air. "I spent the morning sorting out some old magazines, and I'm afraid it tired me more than I thought."

"I can drive you home," Lauren offered. "We're not too busy at the moment and you live just around the block."

"That's kind of you." Mrs. Finch smiled. "I'm sure I'll be all right later on. I'll just sit here with Annie and enjoy my treat."

"We'll get your order ready." Zoe zipped back to the counter.

Lauren made the latte while Zoe plated the gingerbread cupcake.

"Let's ask her about Jay and Kyle," Zoe suggested. "I bet she knows them, or knows someone who knows them."

Mrs. Finch had lived in the small town for many years and had numerous friends and acquaintances.

"Okay," Lauren replied.

"I've had three phone calls today telling me about Annie," Mrs. Finch said as they brought her order over. "How clever you are, dear. You are going to be the star of the Christmas play!"

"Brrt," Annie replied modestly, ducking her head and peeping up from under her lashes.

"Do you know Jay and Kyle?" Zoe asked.

"Who are they?" Mrs. Finch frowned.

"They're new to the town and they're helping out backstage," Lauren replied.

"They live next door to Mrs. Wagner," Zoe prompted.

"Oh." Mrs. Finch's expression cleared. "Yes, I did hear a little something about them. Mrs. Wagner is very upset about her prized rosebush, and I don't blame her. Some young people don't have good manners these days."

Lauren supposed a man in his forties might appear to be young to a woman in her eighties.

"Not either of you, of course, dears," Mrs. Finch added hastily.

Zoe nodded.

"I believe their mother is in assisted living here," Mrs. Finch continued. "Maybe that's why they moved."

"From where?" Zoe asked curiously.

"I'm afraid I don't know." Mrs. Finch picked up her cup with wobbly hands and took a small sip. "Lovely as always." She sighed with pleasure.

After they regretfully cancelled craft club for the following night, they checked that Mrs. Finch had a ticket for the play. She assured them that the senior center minivan would pick her up and take her to the theater. After chatting with her for a couple more minutes, they left her to enjoy her time with Annie.

"I'm glad Jay and Kyle aren't living next door to us," Zoe said as they returned to the counter.

"Me too."

"I just hope they pay Mrs. Wagner for her rosebush like they promised to."

***

That night at the second dress rehearsal, Zoe chewed her lip. The cast waited on stage for Jay to show up.

"I'm sorry, Father Mike," Kyle apologized for his brother. "He said he'd be here tonight."

"I'm sure we can wait a few more minutes for him," Father Mike replied.

"If he takes much longer, surely we can rehearse the scene without him?" Mrs. Wagner tutted. "I would like to get home before midnight."

"Are you going to turn into a pumpkin?" Kyle joked.

Mrs. Wagner glared at him.

"Sorry," he murmured. "I shouldn't have said that."

"No, you should not have, young man," Mrs. Wagner told him frostily.

"Brrt?" Annie asked softly. She sat next to Lauren in the front row of the theater.

Lauren stroked her, the long, fluffy silver-gray fur soft against her fingertips.

"We're waiting for them to change the big painting on the stage." She pointed to the picture of Santa's workshop.

"Brrp." Anne sounded as if she understood.

Father Mike had a bad back at times, and had to be careful, and although Ed had volunteered to change the backdrop, the priest thought maybe they should wait for both brothers.

"Five more minutes," Mrs. Wagner stated, looking at her watch. "And then we should start the next scene – with or without the correct backdrop."

"Agreed." Father Mike glanced over at Annie. "We don't want Annie to stay up too late. Especially if she's working in the café tomorrow."

"Do you think she should have the day off?" Zoe asked, dressed in her head elf costume.

"That might be a good idea," Ed said gruffly, the bell on his hat jangling as he nodded. "So she can rest up for her performance on Saturday night."

"I agree," Lauren said from the front row. "But it really depends on Annie. It's her decision."

"Brrp." Annie tilted her head to the left, and then to the right, as if weighing up the pros and cons. "Brrp."

"I think that means she'll decide later," Lauren told them.

"Brrt!" *That's right!*

"Well, Father." Mrs. Wagner tapped her foot. "I propose—"

"Sorry, Father." Jay burst onto the stage, his face flushed.

"Where were you?" his brother Kyle whispered, a frown on his face. "You've kept everyone waiting."

"Yeah, sorry." Jay didn't look particularly apologetic. "I lost track of time. I had this really good hand and I couldn't waste it – I won ten bucks on it – but then I lost it on the next."

"And where is the money for my rosebush, young man?" Mrs. Wagner demanded.

"I told you you're wasting your time playing online poker." Kyle shook his head. "You'll never learn."

"I think we should get started," Father Mike spoke.

"Yes, or we will never get home tonight." Mrs. Wagner glared at Jay and Kyle.

"Okay, okay," Jay muttered. He and Kyle changed the backdrop.

"Thank you." Father Mike smiled. "Annie, would you like to sit in the sleigh with me?"

"Brrt!" Annie bounded onto the stage and into the sleigh.

"Oops, we forgot to put her hat on!" Zoe ran backstage, returning seconds later with the red Santa hat with white trim.

"I'll do it." How could Lauren have forgotten Annie's costume? She hurried over to the sleigh and gently placed the velvet hat on Annie's head, checking the white trim remained above her fur baby's eyes.

"Brrt." Annie nudged Lauren's hand.

"You're a wonderful Mrs. Claus," Lauren told her softly.

"Brrp," Annie replied just as softly. *Thank you.*

"Places, everyone," Father Mike called out.

Zoe, Ed, and Mrs. Wagner left the stage. Only Annie and Father Mike were in this scene.

Lauren watched the two of them say their lines. She thought Father Mike was the perfect Santa, and of course Annie was the perfect Mrs. Claus. She just hoped everyone who attended the play on Saturday night would feel the same way.

"And now, we'll rehearse the reindeer scene," Father Mike declared.

"Sure thing." Jay said, and with his brother wheeled away the backdrop, only to return a minute later with a reindeer setting.

"Does your mom live in assisted living?" Lauren heard Zoe ask Kyle as she took her place on the stage. Lauren picked up Annie from the sleigh before Jay and Kyle took it away.

"Yes, she does. Near the senior center," Kyle replied.

"Why do you want to know?" Jay asked.

"No reason," Zoe said airily. "Is she coming to see the play?"

"It's all she can talk about." Kyle smiled briefly. "She's really looking forward to it."

"We'll pick her up and take her back when it's over," Jay added.

"I thought we could stop by the supermarket on the way home tonight," Kyle remarked. "We're running low on food."

"Yeah." Jay's glance skittered around the room. "About that. I'm a little short, bro. Can I pay you back?"

"Again?" Kyle sighed. "If you hadn't wasted your money on that poker game—"

"I'm telling you, I'm good at it. It was just a bit of bad luck tonight. If you can't spot me for my share of the groceries, I'll see Mom tomorrow and ask her for a loan."

"You shouldn't bother her with stuff like that." Kyle looked at him askance.

"It's not much. I know she'll lend it to me."

Kyle continued to look at him.

"Fifty bucks will do."

Kyle heaved a sigh. "Okay. I don't want you bothering Mom. But I want it back on payday."

"Yeah, no worries. Thanks, bro." Jay punched his brother in the arm.

Lauren watched them wheel the sleigh off the stage. Had Zoe heard what she had?

Her gaze met Zoe's.

Yep, Zoe's expression seemed to say. *Wait until we get home!*

The rest of the rehearsal ran smoothly.

"I'll see you all tomorrow evening." Father Mike beamed. "Everything went very well tonight. Thank you."

"Not until Jay decided to show up," Mrs. Wagner muttered under her breath.

Lauren and Annie joined Zoe in the dressing room.

"Do you want to take your hat off, Annie?" Lauren asked.

"Brrp." Annie allowed Lauren to remove the hat and put it back in the chest.

"I love playing head elf, but I also love wearing regular clothes again." Zoe pulled on her jeans and purple sweater. "Let's go home. We have a lot to talk about!"

***

Once they arrived home and Lauren had given Annie her supper, consisting of lamb in gravy, they sat down at the kitchen table.

"I think Mrs. Wagner was right about Jay," Zoe declared as she sipped a glass of orange juice. "He should have paid her back for the rose bush he destroyed instead of playing online poker."

"I agree," Lauren replied, as she drank some water.

"I have no idea why Jay and Kyle are even participating backstage." Zoe's eyes widened. "Do you think they're being forced to, because it's community service or something?"

Lauren stared at her. "Do you think they're criminals?"

"Not exactly, but what if they got into a bit of trouble and they're paying their dues? Maybe they're doing community service so they don't go to jail!"

"I wonder if Mitch knows," Lauren mused, then shook her head. "Isn't it more likely that they're new in town and they wanted to help the community?"

Zoe scoffed. "Maybe Kyle, but I can't see Jay doing this out of the goodness of his heart, can you? Not from the little we know about him."

"It *is* Christmas," Lauren pointed out. "Maybe he wants to do something nice for Father Mike, and the town."

"I wonder where he works." Zoe drummed her fingers on the pine table.

"Brrt?" Annie jumped up on the chair next to Lauren's.

"Do you know where Jay works, Annie?" Zoe asked.

Annie seemed to think about it.

"Brrp," she finally said.

"I think that means no." Lauren stroked the silver-gray tabby's shoulder.

"We could check with Father Mike," Zoe commented. "He must know something. I mean, how did Jay and Kyle even find out about the Christmas play?"

"By seeing one of the posters Father Mike put up asking for volunteers?"

"Good point." Zoe sipped her juice. "I guess we'll have to wait until tomorrow to find out more. I'll ask Father Mike as soon as I see him!"

CHAPTER 4

Father Mike came into the café the next morning a few minutes after they'd opened.

"Hi, Lauren, and Zoe." He smiled at them. "Hi, Annie."

Annie ran to greet him.

"Look what I've bought for Mrs. Snuggle." He pulled out a stuffed, furry brown squirrel. It looked very squishy. "It has catnip in it. Do you think she'll like it?"

"I'm sure she'll love it," Lauren assured him.

"Definitely," Zoe agreed.

"Brrt!" *Yes!*

"It's for her Christmas stocking," he told them. "I want her to enjoy her first Christmas with me."

"I'm sure she will," Lauren replied.

"Do you know much about Jay and Kyle?" Zoe asked as Lauren took his order.

"Not really," Father Mike replied. "Their mother is in assisted living in town, and they recently moved to be closer to her. I think they're from LA. Why?"

"I was just curious," Zoe told him.

"It's kind of them to help out with the play," Father Mike continued. "I'm afraid I didn't get a big response from my posters asking for volunteers."

"That's terrible," Zoe said indignantly.

"People are busy at Christmas," Father Mike said philosophically. "But I think it would be a shame if I stopped putting on the play each year."

"Yes, it would be," Lauren replied, feeling guilty for not assisting more this year.

"You can put my name down to play head elf next year," Zoe told him.

"And I can help out more backstage."

"Brrt!" *And I can play Mrs. Claus again!*

"That would be wonderful." Father Mike beamed at all of them. "Thank you."

Lauren prepared his order while Zoe chatted to him. Then Annie led him to the table she'd chosen for him.

"I didn't get a chance to ask anything else about Jay and Kyle." Zoe frowned.

Lauren glanced over at Annie and Father Mike. The Norwegian Forest Cat kept him company as he drank his latte and enjoyed his gingerbread cupcake.

"He was telling me about Mrs. Snuggle, and how he thinks she's starting to settle in," Zoe said.

"I hope she hasn't scratched him again," Lauren said.

"Me too." Zoe snapped her fingers. "Oh, guess what? Father Mike just said the play has sold out!"

***

On Saturday night, the small theater was packed – standing room only. Lauren and Zoe peeked out from behind the crimson velvet drapes. All their friends and regular customers were in the audience, including Claire, her husband, and little Molly, Martha and her pals from the senior center, Mrs. Finch, Hans, and Ms. Tobin. Brooke and Jeff sat in the third row.

Jay and Kyle had escorted an elderly lady to a seat near the front – Lauren assumed she was their mother. She was a little unsteady on her feet, despite hanging on to both men's arms.

Chris had helped out at the final dress rehearsal last night, Zoe's face lighting up when she saw him. Mitch stopped by the cottage afterward, and the four of them enjoyed the cupcakes Lauren had saved from the café.

Now, Mitch and Chris sat in the front row, saving a seat for Lauren.

Lauren wanted to watch the play from the audience, but she also needed to be backstage for Annie – and Zoe.

Mitch had promised to record the show for AJ and Toby, Annie's feline friends.

"I think I should stay backstage," she told Zoe, who was already dressed in her elf costume.

Annie wore her lavender harness, standing quietly by Lauren's side, her green eyes wide as she watched the cast bustle past, getting ready for the first scene.

"At least for Annie's first scene," Zoe agreed. "Maybe you and Annie could watch the rest from the front row until it's time for her to go on again."

"Good idea." Lauren smiled. Annie could sit in her lap.

"Is everyone ready?" Father Mike appeared in his Santa outfit, looking harried. "I do like starting on time."

"I am, Father." Mrs. Wagner spoke from behind him. "As you can see, I'm ready to go on." She gestured to her green and white elf costume.

"Wonderful." The priest smiled at her. "Where is Ed? And Jay and Kyle?"

"Here, Father." Ed's gruff voice sounded from the wings. He jammed the elf hat onto his head, the bell jangling.

Father Mike scratched his white cotton wool beard. "How are we going to change the scenery between acts if Jay and Kyle aren't here?"

"Mitch and Chris might be able to help with that," Lauren suggested.

"That would be a wonderful solution." Relief flickered across Father Mike's face.

"I'll go now and ask them." She handed Annie's harness to Zoe. "But I saw Jay and Kyle with an older lady in the audience – maybe she's their mom?"

"Sorry we're late." Kyle and his brother Jay jogged into view.

"We brought Mom to see the play," Jay said.

"We were just getting her settled," Kyle added.

"Not to worry." Father Mike nodded. "I think we should get started." He gestured to the stage curtain blocking them from the view of the audience.

Zoe handed Annie's harness back to Lauren and suddenly clutched her stomach.

"I think I'm going to be sick!"

Lauren stared at her. She'd never suspected that Zoe might suffer from stage fright, while she on the other hand …

"Brrt?" Annie peered up at her.

"My tummy feels really weird," Zoe told her.

"It's okay, Zoe," Father Mike told her gently. "We have time if you need to go to the bathroom. It happens to a lot of people."

"It's not supposed to happen to me!"

"Amateurs." Mrs. Wagner tutted, shaking her head.

70

Zoe's nostrils flared and she straightened her spine.

"I feel fine, Father," Zoe declared after a few seconds. "Perfectly fine."

"If you're sure." He looked at her doubtfully.

"Let's get started!" Zoe took her place on the stage.

"Okay."

The rest of the cast took their places. The curtain rose.

Lauren and Annie watched from the wings. She glanced at Annie, noting the cat's wide-eyed look of wonder as Father Mike, Zoe, Mrs. Wagner, and Ed spoke their lines perfectly and moved around the stage, the audience laughing when appropriate.

"It will be your turn soon," she whispered to Annie.

"Brrp," Annie replied just as softly.

The applause was loud as the curtain closed.

"That was wonderful, everyone!" Father Mike beamed at the small cast. "Now, Annie, are you ready to be Mrs. Claus?"

"Brrt!" *Yes!*

"Let me put on your hat." Lauren had it in her purse, and bent down and placed it on Annie's head, making sure the white trim at the base didn't obscure her vision.

"Brrp." *Thank you.*

"You're going to be the best Mrs. Claus ever," Lauren whispered to her.

Annie nudged her hand as Lauren unbuckled the lavender harness.

"She'll be perfectly fine, Lauren." Father Mike seemed to understand her sudden anxiety.

It had seemed a great idea to have Annie take part in the play but now Lauren suddenly fretted about what could go wrong.

What if the size of the audience scared Annie? She was used to people coming and going in the café, but not a crowd as big as this one.

What if the applause frightened her and she ran off the stage?

"Brrt." *I'll be fine.* Annie nudged her hand again.

Lauren took a deep breath.

"Okay."

Annie jumped into the sleigh. Father Mike clambered in after her.

"It's going to be perfect," Zoe murmured. "Just wait and see."

The curtain rose.

A burst of applause sounded in the small space as the audience caught their first glimpse of Annie.

Father Mike leaned back so everyone could see the silver-gray tabby sitting in the sleigh.

"Annie!" Molly called from near the front of the audience, her chubby hands waving in the air. "Annie!"

"Brrt!" Annie replied, peering sideways in front of Father Mike, her furry face alive with pleasure. "Brrt!" *Hello!*

The audience laughed. Once they settled down, Lauren could hear them talking to each other.

"I didn't think it would be possible!"

"I know!"

"She's such a lovely cat."

"She's definitely helped out Father Mike by taking part."

Father Mike waited until the chatter died away, then with a smile on his face, spoke his first line for the scene.

"Well, Mrs. Claus, do you think we have enough presents for all the good boys and girls?"

"Brrt!" *Yes!*

"Pwesent for Molly?" Molly called out anxiously.

The audience laughed, and Molly looked around with wide eyes, her little cheeks flushed.

"Brrt!" Annie replied.

"Yes, I think we *do* have a present for Molly," Father Mike improvised. "I'm sure she's been a very good girl this year."

"Yeah!" Molly cheered.

Lauren saw Claire kiss her daughter and whisper in her ear. Molly settled down in her seat, a big smile on her face.

"I've been good, too!" a boy yelled from the middle of the audience.

"I'm sure you have been, Peter," Father Mike said gravely. "Now, Mrs. Claus, let's deliver these gifts to children all over the world. We must hurry, or else we won't finish before dawn."

"Ooh!" Molly's mouth parted.

"Brrt!" Annie said her line.

"Wait, Santa!" Zoe ran onto the stage as head elf. "Do you have all the toys?"

"Zoe!" Molly called out.

"Hi, Molly!" Zoe turned and waved at the little girl. She followed Father Mike in improvising. "I must finish this special job for Santa right away!"

Molly's eyes grew even bigger.

The rest of the scene flowed smoothly, with no more interruptions from the audience.

To Lauren's relief, the applause and interactions from the audience didn't seem to faze Annie at all. By the time the scene ended, Lauren had a smile on her face. Father Mike definitely knew how to write a lovely Christmas play.

"Yay!" the kids cheered as the curtain closed on Annie, Father Mike, and Zoe. "Yay!"

"You were wonderful," Lauren told Annie as the feline hopped from the sleigh into Lauren's arms.

Annie's green eyes sparkled as she snuggled into Lauren.

"Brrt." *Thank you.*

"Everyone is going to talk about tonight." Zoe grinned. "Even more now that they've seen Annie on stage."

"I think you're right," Father Mike agreed.

"You did very well, Annie." Mrs. Wagner came up to them.

"Brrt." Annie blinked modestly.

"Let's get ready for the next scene, everyone," Father Mike told them.

"Annie and I will sit in the audience," Lauren said. "Mitch saved me a seat."

"Have fun." Zoe beamed at them.

"You're an amazing head elf," Lauren told her cousin.

"Thanks!"

There was a buzz in the crowd as Lauren made her way to the front row, Annie in her arms.

Mitch smiled at her, and made sure she and Annie were settled comfortably, Annie sitting demurely in her lap.

"You were great, Annie," Mitch murmured.

"Brrt!" *Thank you.*

"Definitely." Chris nodded, as he sat on Lauren's other side.

"Brrt!"

"Isn't Annie in it anymore?" A child's voice wailed from the middle of the theater.

The curtain rose. This scene featured the naughty elf played by Ed, stealing the toys.

This time, there were no interruptions from the audience who seemed delighted at the conclusion, with the mischievous elf made to clean the reindeer stables every day for the next year, as well as keeping the sleigh spick and span.

Then, it was time for Annie to appear in the final scene with Father Mike, sitting in the sleigh. It went off without a hitch, all the children in the audience cheering when Annie appeared on stage again.

When the curtain closed for the last time, everyone cheered.

"Awesome!"

"That was wonderful!"

"Even better than last year. Annie really stole the show!"

Lauren heard the audience's comments and kissed the top of Annie's head. She was so proud of her fur baby.

Lauren and Mitch found it hard to go backstage, as practically everyone wanted to congratulate Annie on their way out of the theater.

"Saw you, Annie!" Molly beamed as she held onto her mother's hand. "Up there!" She pointed to the stage.

"Brrt." *That's right.*

"You were wonderful, Annie," Claire told her. Her husband wrapped his arm around her.

"Never seen anything like it," he said.

"Hi, cutie pie." Martha rolled to a stop in front of them and winked at Annie. "That was terrific. You'll have to take part again next year, or the whole town might stage a protest!"

"Do you think?" Lauren asked, crinkling her brow.

"Definitely." Martha nodded vigorously.

"Would you like that?" Lauren murmured to Annie.

"Brrt!" *Yes!*

"We'll have to talk to Father Mike about it next Christmas," Lauren replied.

Lauren and Mitch waited until the crowd dispersed. Chris had made a break for it and gone backstage.

"I recorded the whole thing," Mitch said, tapping his phone. "I'll send you a copy."

"Thanks," Lauren replied with a smile. "I'll email a copy to Ed so AJ can watch it, and one to Toby's owner, Jerry."

They finally made their way backstage and headed to the dressing room.

Lauren heard Zoe's animated voice before she saw her.

"Do you think my improvised dialogue was okay when Molly called out to me?"

"It was perfect," Chris's reassuring voice from inside the room.

"Oh, good. And what did you think about …"

Lauren turned away.

"Maybe we should give them some time alone," she suggested to Mitch.

Mrs. Wagner came out of the dressing room, dressed in her regular clothes of a navy jacket and matching pants.

"I don't think there's much privacy in there," he replied.

Ed walked out of the dressing room next, wearing a flannel shirt and faded jeans.

"I'll send you the recording that Mitch made," Lauren told him. "You were great."

"Thanks," he replied gruffly. "I'm glad to get that hat off – all that jangling reminded me of AJ's jingle ball she likes playing with."

Lauren laughed.

Zoe and Chris came out of the dressing room, Zoe dressed in her usual outfit of jeans and a sweater – this time red with purple zigzags.

"I'm definitely going to play head elf next year," Zoe declared. "It was so much fun!"

"Thank you, everyone." Father Mike approached. "You're a natural, Annie. I'm sure Mrs. Snuggle will be interested to hear about tonight. I'll tell her how the play went as soon as I get home."

"Do you need a hand cleaning up, Father?" Mitch asked. "Chris and I can help out."

"Thank you," the priest replied. "That's very kind. Jay and Kyle had to take their mother back to the senior home. So I've decided I'll clean up on Monday, as I have church services tomorrow."

"Oh, that's right," Lauren said guiltily. She'd forgotten about that, although she and Zoe didn't attend every week.

"It's all right, Lauren," Father Mike said kindly. "You and Annie have really helped me out – as well as the rest of the cast. I'm sure Annie would like to sleep late tomorrow."

"Thanks, Father."

"I can come over and help after work on Monday," Mitch said.

"The café's closed on Monday, so Zoe and I can be here as well," Lauren offered.

"Me too," Chris said. "I have an early shift on Monday so I should be free late afternoon."

"Wonderful!" Father Mike beamed at them. "With so many people here, we'll get this place cleaned up in a jiffy!"

They said goodnight to Father Mike and headed to Lauren's cottage.

Mitch walked Lauren and Annie to the porch, the warm golden light shining above them.

"I'll see you tomorrow," he murmured, placing a kiss on her forehead.

Annie nestled in her arms, her eyes closed. A soft sigh sounded, as if she was having a lovely dream.

"I hope this hasn't been too much for her," Lauren said. "I know she enjoyed herself, but—"

"I'm sure she'll be fine," Mitch replied reassuringly. "And she's got all day tomorrow and Monday to relax."

"And all of next week if that's what she wants," Lauren added. Annie was free to come and go from the café to the cottage all day long, but she usually chose to assist with the customers.

"Of course." Mitch kissed her softly. "You're a great mom."

"Thanks." Heat hit her cheeks. What would it be like if she and Mitch got married and had children one day? She gazed up at him, *hoping he could not read her thoughts right now.*

He unlocked the door for her, as she still held Annie, and turned on the living room light.

She watched Zoe exit Chris's car and hurry up the porch steps.

"Don't shut me out," she teased. "I need my beauty sleep!"

CHAPTER 5

At breakfast, Zoe chattered to Lauren and Annie about her date with Chris.

"Since you and Mitch are having lunch here, Chris is taking me out for our own date," she stated, crunching buttery toast as she spoke.

"Where are you going?" Lauren asked, glad that Chris had a day off and was spending it with her cousin.

"We haven't decided yet," Zoe admitted. "But I get to choose. I'm thinking about that ice cream place in Sacramento but I don't know whether I want to drive for an hour just to get some ice cream, even if it is amazing."

"I hear you." Lauren nodded. Even though it was winter, she still enjoyed the frozen treat – and knew Zoe did, too.

"Maybe somewhere more local," her cousin mused. "Or maybe I'll just make some sandwiches and we can go hiking in the forest. It's not too cold to do that, and if the temperature drops, Chris can keep me warm." She winked at Lauren and Annie.

"Brrt?" Annie asked, bunting Lauren's arm. She hadn't woken when Lauren had gently placed her on her bed, and had slept all night. Now, however, she seemed her usual energetic self.

"We've both got dates today, Annie," Zoe told her. "Mitch is coming over here and spending time with Lauren."

"I thought you'd like a relaxing day at home," Lauren added. "You've been very busy with the play."

"Brrp."

"You're welcome to join me and Mitch," Lauren offered. "I don't know what he's got planned, though."

"What about a video play date with AJ?" Zoe suggested. "You could tell her all about last night!"

"Brrt!" Annie's eyes lit up.

"Why don't I set that up now?" Lauren hurried into the living room to grab her phone.

"Do you think Ed is up yet?" Zoe asked.

"I hope so." Lauren checked her watch as she re-entered the kitchen. "It's nine o'clock."

"Yeah, he should be awake."

Ed came into the café even earlier than they did some days, to get a jump start on his pastries.

"Maybe you can have a video play date with Toby later today," Zoe said.

"Brrt!" *Yes!* Annie placed her paw on the phone, and pressed a button.

The screen flickered, then came to life.

"Brrp." Annie pressed another button and they heard a buzz.

She'd called AJ all by herself previously, something Lauren still marveled at.

"Meow?" A brown furry face peered at them from the screen, a darker brown M on her forehead.

"Hi, AJ," Lauren spoke to the Maine Coon tabby.

"Brrt!" Annie greeted her friend.

"Hi Ed," Zoe called out.

"Hi," Ed's gruff voice sounded. "Is Annie calling AJ?"

"Yes. Is this a good time?" Lauren asked.

"Sure. Do you want to play with Annie?" she heard him ask AJ.

"Meow!"

"I'll set AJ up in the living room. Hang on."

"Brrt!" Annie ran to *their* living room, looking back over her shoulder at Lauren.

"I'm coming." Lauren jogged after her, carrying the phone. Annie would have more room for her play date in that room, and easy access to her toys. Sometimes she and AJ showed each other their playthings over the phone.

"Brrt!" Lauren heard her fur baby speak to AJ as she headed back to the kitchen.

"I wonder if Mrs. Snuggle will ever want to do a play date like that," Zoe mused as she finished eating her toast.

"Or any play date at all," Lauren added. The Persian hadn't seemed interested in making friends with Annie a couple of months ago, but now she was living with Father Mike, perhaps she would want to, one day.

"We should go and visit her," Zoe suggested. "See how she's getting on with Father Mike."

"Good idea," Lauren replied. "We could take her a little Christmas gift."

"Something else for her stocking." Zoe grinned.

They spent the rest of the morning doing light housework and getting ready for their dates.

Lauren stood in front of her bedroom mirror, wondering what to wear. Mitch said he would organize something, but she wasn't sure what he had in mind. Should she wear a casual outfit or something a little dressier?

"What do you think, Annie?" Her fur baby had finished playing with AJ over the phone, and had jumped up on the bed, looking at her inquiringly.

"This or this?"

Lauren held out the two outfits. One featured fawn slacks with a plum sweater. The other consisted of jeans with a navy wrap top.

Zoe was getting dressed for her own date with Chris, otherwise Lauren would have asked for her opinion as well.

"Brrt!" Annie lifted her left paw.

"This one?" Lauren indicated the fawn and plum combination.

"Brrt!" *Yes.*

"I think you're right." Lauren smiled. Zoe had told her a while ago that plum looked good with her light brown hair with hints of natural gold, and the sweater skimmed her curves nicely. The outfit wasn't too dressy but not too casual, either.

"What do you think?" Zoe barged into the bedroom and twirled.

"Zoe!" Lauren didn't know whether to laugh.

Her cousin wore jeans, and a green and purple sweater.

"I decided we should go hiking." Zoe's brown eyes sparkled. "After we have burgers at Gary's."

"Good choice." Lauren nodded.

"I think Mitch should have told you what he had in mind for today, so you could dress appropriately."

"I think this outfit covers most options." She pointed at the fawn slacks and plum sweater. "Annie seems to think it's what I should wear."

"Good eye, Annie." Zoe winked at the silver-gray tabby. "Hey, if you and Mitch go out, you could set up Annie's play date with Toby before you leave."

"Just what I was thinking." Lauren smiled. "Would you like that, Annie?"

"Brrt!" *Yes!*

Lauren finished getting ready, half listening to Zoe muse about which part of the Tahoe National Park she wanted to explore, and wondering what Mitch had in mind for today. She didn't really care, as long as they spent some time together. Did he feel the same way?

The doorbell rang.

"I wonder if that's Chris – or Mitch?" Zoe zoomed to the front door.

"Hi, Chris."

Lauren smiled as she heard the pleasure in her cousin's voice.

"Yes, I'm ready," she heard Zoe say.

Zoe poked her head back in Lauren's bedroom. "I'm going now. You two have fun!"

"You too."

"Brrt!"

Lauren heard the front door slam.

"Mitch should be here soon," she told Annie, wondering why he hadn't arrived with Chris, since they were currently roommates.

Lauren sat on the bed and gathered Annie in her arms. They just cuddled together, enjoying the closeness and the silence of the house for a few minutes.

The doorbell rang.

"That must be Mitch." Lauren gently placed Annie on the bed.

Annie hopped down and followed Lauren.

"Hi." Lauren opened the front door.

"Hi." Mitch smiled at her. Dressed in jeans and a blue sweater, his good looks made her heart flutter.

He held out a large bag. "I thought we could have lunch here. I brought everything we need, including that Zinfandel you liked from the local winery."

"That sounds perfect."

"Brrt!" Annie agreed.

CHAPTER 6

Lauren enjoyed her lunch – and afternoon – with Mitch. She thought Annie did too, although the feline left them halfway through the date for her own playtime with Toby over the phone. She'd made friends with the golden Siberian Forest cat a couple of months ago at a local cat show, and they'd stayed in touch.

Mitch had brought sourdough bread, cheese, green salad, freshly sliced ham, and chocolate mousse – as well as a bottle of Lauren's favorite wine.

"I thought this would give you a break from making something for us," he told her as they sat in the kitchen. "And we could have some time to ourselves."

"Zoe's date with Chris …?" Suspicion dawned.

"He'd planned on seeing her today, anyway." Mitch smiled. "If Zoe had decided to have their date here, we could have gone to the National Park instead – or even my place."

Lauren hadn't been to Mitch's apartment much – he seemed to prefer visiting her. And now Chris had moved in with him temporarily, it seemed a less likely spot to hang out.

"I'm sorry I haven't given us enough time lately." Mitch captured her hand across the table. "I've allowed myself to be pulled in too many different directions with work, and catching up with Chris. But you know I'm here one hundred percent for you – and Annie. Don't you?"

"I do now." Warmth flowed through her at his words, and the feel of her hand in his. "Thank you."

He kissed the palm of her hand.

"You're all I want, Lauren." He cleared his throat. "I don't think I tell you that enough."

Lauren's eyes grew misty.

"You're all I want, too."

Lauren couldn't look away from him, wishing this moment could go on forever. Then Annie cantered into the room, carrying her toy hedgehog in her mouth. She dropped it at Lauren's feet.

"Brrt!"

***

After playing with Annie, Lauren and Mitch went for a walk. Annie accompanied them in her harness.

"I'll see you tomorrow at the theater." Mitch kissed her tenderly that evening.

"Yes."

Zoe and Chris had arrived home around dinner time, carrying two pizzas, which they'd all shared. Then Chris made his apologies and left, citing an early shift in the morning.

It was a shame Mitch had to work tomorrow, otherwise they could have done something together before heading to the town hall to help Father Mike clean up.

She waved goodbye to him as he headed down the porch steps. She was so ready to tell him she loved him – but she wasn't sure why she'd held back today. Maybe she was subconsciously waiting for him to say it first? But his heartfelt words – and actions – were enough for her right now.

"Chris and I had so much fun today." Zoe grinned as Lauren entered the living

94

room. "I just wish he didn't have to start work early in the morning."

"I hear you." Lauren nodded.

"Maybe we can all have dinner together after we help Father Mike tomorrow," Zoe continued.

"Good idea."

"I just wish there were more dining options in town," Zoe added. "There's Gary's Burger Diner, and the pizza place, but the steakhouse is closed on Mondays and so is the bistro."

"There's the Italian in Zeke's Ridge," Lauren suggested, "but I'm not sure if it's open on Monday."

"Ooh, yes!" Zoe's eyes lit up. "But are we going to want to drive over there after spending a couple of hours cleaning up? That's if it *is* open."

"Probably not," Lauren said ruefully, thinking of having to get up early on Tuesday to bake cupcakes and open the café on time.

"Hey!" Zoe snapped her fingers. "Maybe the guys can cook for us! At Mitch's apartment!"

"I love that idea." Lauren smiled. "But can they cook?"

"You've been dating Mitch for over a year and you don't know if he can cook?" Zoe's eyebrows climbed to the top of her brunette pixie bangs.

"He's good with steak," Lauren offered. "And he can put together a picnic." She blushed at the memory of his words yesterday. *'You're all I want.'*

"Chris can cook some things," Zoe told her. "But I don't think he's as good as you."

"Thanks."

"He makes a great chili," Zoe continued. "Maybe he could make that for us."

"Doesn't chili take a long time if you do it right?" Lauren asked. She'd only ever made a quick version with ground beef.

"I forgot about that." Zoe tapped her cheek. "Yeah, I remember him telling me once he likes to cook it long and slow."

"Maybe we should opt for burgers or pizza," Lauren said. "I'm not going to feel like making dinner tomorrow night."

"Me neither," Zoe replied.

Lauren stifled a smile – Zoe didn't do much cooking. One of her favorite homemade meals was left over Paninis from the cafe.

They decided to go to bed early.

"We've got our grocery shopping tomorrow, and we should check on Mrs. Finch," Lauren reminded her.

"That's right." Zoe looked guilty. "We didn't stop by her house today."

"I'm sure she'll understand." They'd seen their friend the previous night, and she'd seemed fine.

"And then we could visit Mrs. Snuggle," Zoe suggested.

"And buy a little toy for her."

"Brrt!"

CHAPTER 7

The next morning, Lauren and Zoe visited the supermarket, and then Mrs. Finch. They had a lovely time chatting with her about Annie's success on Saturday night, and made her a coffee using her pod machine.

"Now we should drop by Father Mike's," Zoe suggested, "and give Mrs. Snuggle her gift from us."

"And Annie," Lauren reminded her.

"That's right."

They'd bought a gray, furry mouse for the Persian.

They drove to the parsonage, a white clapboard house next to the church.

Ding dong.

The front door bell chimed within the depths of the house.

"Lauren – and Zoe." Father Mike beamed at them as he opened the door. He was dressed down in a pair of old jeans and a blue sweater. "What a nice surprise."

"We bought a little something for Mrs. Snuggle." Zoe waved the mouse in the air.

"We didn't have time to giftwrap it." Lauren had completely forgotten about doing that.

"No worries. It's such a kind thought. Please, come in."

They entered the hallway, the walls painted a light gray.

Father Mike led them to the living room, decorated in shades of cream and pale green, where Mrs. Snuggle reposed on an elderly khaki sofa. Her plush white fur looked showstopping against a cozy red blanket. Her blue eyes looked at them curiously for a second, before narrowing into slits, then closing. It appeared she'd decided to ignore them.

"I've been telling Mrs. Snuggle all about Christmas," he said. "I've hung up her stocking already." He gestured to the mantel where a red, white, and green stocking was displayed. "I'll wait until Christmas Eve before I put her present in."

"Now you have two gifts for her." Zoe handed him the mouse, then paused. "Do you think she's watching? I didn't mean to spoil her surprise." She glanced at the Persian, who continued to ignore all of them.

"I thought she might say hello to you." Father Mike looked embarrassed. "I'm sorry. I don't think she's as social as Annie."

"Maybe it takes her a while to warm up to strangers," Lauren offered.

"I think that must be it." Father Mike nodded. "But I'm sure she likes living with me a little more now. She hasn't scratched me for weeks and has stopped hissing at me."

"That's good." Lauren didn't know what else to say.

"Maybe one day she can be friends with Annie," Father Mike's tone was wistful. "And AJ."

"We can set up a play date for them," Lauren replied, "when you think Mrs. Snuggle is ready."

"It could be a video one, or an in-person one," Zoe added. "Whatever you think is best."

"Thank you." Father Mike smiled. "I'm sure Mrs. Snuggle would like that, when she's ready to make friends."

***

Mid-afternoon, they walked over to the theater. Lauren had already mixed up two batches of cupcake batter at the café, ready to be baked in the morning. Now, they were going to help Father Mike clean up after Saturday's production.

"I wonder if Chris will be there already," Zoe pondered as they opened the unlocked stage door.

"And Mitch."

"And Jay and Kyle." Zoe looked doubtful.

"Did they promise Father Mike they'd help clean up, too?"

"I'm not sure. But can we really count on them to keep their word, anyway?" Zoe scrunched her face.

"Good point." Lauren tried to think the best of people, but she wasn't sure about the brothers, especially Jay.

"They haven't visited the café, have they?"

"No."

"I wonder where they work." Zoe tapped her cheek. "We still don't know."

They entered backstage and surveyed the darkened space.

"Hello?" Lauren called out.

"Is there anyone here?" Zoe added.

Silence.

"It looks like we're the first ones," Lauren commented.

"Let's check the dressing room." Zoe headed toward that area, her footsteps echoing on the wooden floorboards. "Maybe Father Mike is already there, tidying up the costumes."

Lauren followed her cousin, a sinking feeling in the pit of her stomach. The silence seemed eerie, and all the lights were off, apart from a dim bulb in the corner near the dressing room. If Father Mike were here, wouldn't the lights be on?

"Maybe we should go outside and wait for someone else to show up." She touched Zoe's arm.

"I'm sure Father Mike won't mind if we start without him – and the others." Zoe continued to the dressing room. "In

102

fact, sorting through the costumes is a good idea. I don't think we'd be able to move the backdrops – I thought we could leave that to the guys."

Lauren reluctantly followed her cousin, the uneasy feeling growing.

"Father Mike, are you in here?" Zoe pushed open the dressing room door.

Lauren noticed it had been ajar.

"Nope." Zoe shook her head.

The overhead light shone in the room, highlighting costumes strewn everywhere.

"That's strange." Zoe frowned. "When I got dressed after the show on Saturday, the outfits weren't scattered all over the room. I hung mine up on the rack." She pointed to a metal railing that held only one costume – Father Mike's red and white Santa outfit.

"I think we should go outside and wait for the others," Lauren suggested again. Something just didn't feel right.

She swung around, heading for the door, when she saw a hand on the floor, underneath a pile of elf costumes. It looked like a man's hand.

"Zoe …"

"What?" Zoe's expression changed as she realized there was *a tone* in Lauren's voice. "Can you see something?"

"There." Lauren pointed at the hand.

"Father Mike!" they both exclaimed. They rushed over to the costumes and flung them away, to reveal …

Jay.

Blood seeped through his gray sweater around his stomach. He looked pale … and dead.

"I'm calling for help." Lauren dug her phone out of her purse. Thank goodness Annie had stayed at home – she didn't need to see this. Lauren turned away from the prone figure, feeling sick.

"Maybe he's not dead," she heard Zoe say, while she waited for the operator.

"Oh. I think he is."

She swiveled to watch Zoe gently place his hand back on the ground.

"Chris showed me how to take a pulse," she explained.

"Have we got a compact?" Lauren asked. They'd used that method before to check if someone was breathing.

"I only brought my wallet with me," Zoe admitted.

Lauren spoke to the operator, outlining the situation as best she could. "Help is on the way," she told her cousin.

"Hey, Jay, I got the burgers." Kyle walked into the room, dressed in winter wear and a scarf, and froze. "What's going on?"

"I don't know how to tell you this," Lauren replied awkwardly. "But I think your brother is dead."

CHAPTER 8

Kyle stared at them, dropping the big paper bag he carried with a *thunk*.

"What?"

"Over there." Zoe pointed to Jay's body.

"Jay!" Kyle rushed to his brother and lifted his head. "No!"

"Um, I don't think we're supposed to touch anything." Lauren bit her lip.

"Yes, you don't want to contaminate the crime scene."

"Crime scene?" Kyle looked bewildered. "What are you talking about?"

"He's got a lot of blood on him." Zoe pointed again to Jay.

"I've called the authorities," Lauren told him. "Help is coming."

Sirens sounded in the street.

"Oh, good." Zoe looked just as relieved as Lauren felt.

"I'm really sorry, Kyle."

"Me too," Zoe added.

"What happened?" Kyle crouched beside his brother and looked up at them. "Did you see anything? I went to get burgers for us before I joined him here as we didn't have time for lunch today. He said he'd be fine here on his own."

"We just got here," Lauren replied.

"Yeah, there was no one else around," Zoe added. "Ed is helping out at the senior center today and wasn't able to make it."

Two paramedics arrived, followed by Chris.

"I was just finishing my shift when we got the call," he told Zoe. "Are you okay?"

"I'm fine." She looked pleased to see him.

"Lauren?" Chris turned to her.

"I'll be okay." She took a deep breath. What she really wanted to do was go outside and get some cold, fresh air.

"I called Mitch and he's on his way," Chris added.

"Thanks." Lauren nodded.

Lauren watched one of the paramedics shake his head. Kyle stood to the side, looking devastated.

"Lauren." Mitch strode inside.

"Mitch."

He put his arm around her shoulders. "Tell me what happened."

"Do you think we could go outside?"

"Sure." He guided her to the theater exit.

Lauren took grateful breaths of air and leaned against the chilly brick wall of the town hall. Why did she and Zoe keep finding dead bodies? She didn't even want to know how many they'd stumbled across in the past.

"Better?" Mitch looked at her in concern.

She nodded. After a minute, she told him exactly what she'd witnessed.

"So you haven't seen Father Mike today?"

"Not since we stopped by his house around lunchtime to give Mrs. Snuggle a Christmas gift."

His mouth quirked slightly, then he sobered.

"I know he was coming to the theater this afternoon to clean up after Saturday night," Lauren continued. "At first, I thought Zoe and I were the first ones to arrive, and then I saw Jay's ..." her voice trailed off.

Mitch wrapped his arms around her and held her close.

"Thanks." Her voice was muffled against his navy jacket.

"Are you okay?" Zoe came out of the building, followed by Chris.

"I'll be fine." Lauren straightened her shoulders. "I just wasn't expecting to see Jay like that."

"Yeah," Zoe said with feeling. "Chris thinks he was stabbed in the stomach."

"Really?" Mitch glanced at his friend.

"It looks that way from what I saw," Chris explained. "But you'll know for sure once you get the medical examiner's report."

"I'll have to go back inside and question Kyle," Mitch said. "I was about to clock off in thirty minutes and come over to help clean up here. Then we got the call."

"At least Detective Castern isn't around," Zoe said. "You'll be in charge of the case – won't you?"

"Probably." Mitch nodded.

He went back inside to interview Kyle.

"I guess we have to hang around until Mitch finishes in there," Zoe said. "Did you tell him what we saw?" She turned to Lauren.

"Yes." Lauren still felt a little shaky.

"Why don't I check with Mitch and see if you two can go home?" Chris suggested. "He'll know where to find you."

"That would be great," Lauren replied.

"Ooh – we'll have to call Father Mike and tell him not to come here," Zoe said. "He doesn't need to get caught up in this."

"Agreed," Lauren replied.

Chris texted Mitch while Zoe called Father Mike.

After a minute, Chris nodded as he looked at his phone screen.

"Mitch says that's fine."

"Good." Lauren smiled slightly.

"Bye, Father Mike." Zoe ended her phone call.

"He was just about to come over," she told them. "He sounded really shocked."

"I *am* really shocked," Lauren said, leaning against the brick wall.

"Chris, do you want to come home with us or hang out here with Mitch?" Zoe asked.

"I'll go back to the cottage with you two, if that's okay with Lauren," he replied.

"Of course it is," Lauren replied.

"We don't have any cupcakes." Zoe frowned.

"But I can make you a latte," Lauren offered. She had a home espresso machine in the cottage kitchen.

"I think we all need one." Zoe brightened.

They piled into Chris's car for the short drive to their house.

When they arrived, Annie ran to greet them.

"Brrt?" she enquired, an inquisitive expression on her face.

"Another murder, Annie," Zoe told her.

"Zoe!" Lauren preferred her fur baby not to have to think about things like that. Although Annie seemed to sense something had gone awry, Lauren would have tried to break the news to her more gently.

111

"It was Jay, who helped backstage for the Christmas play," she murmured to Annie.

"Brrp." She looked thoughtful, then led the way to the living room.

Annie hopped up on the sofa, turned around in a circle, and settled down.

"We're going to make lattes," Zoe told her.

Lauren sat down next to the Norwegian Forest Cat and gently stroked her.

"I'm sure Mitch will figure out who did it," she said reassuringly. "There's nothing for you to worry about."

"And if he doesn't, we will," Zoe declared.

***

The next morning, Lauren and Zoe unstacked the pine chairs in the café. Annie sat in her basket, 'supervising'.

"So what did Mitch say last night?" Zoe snooped.

"When he called me later?"

"Yes."

Mitch had arrived around dinner time, his face somber. Lauren had thrown together some pasta with spaghetti sauce, which the guys had wolfed down.

Then Mitch said he had to go back to the station to catch up on paperwork, but he'd call her that evening. Which he did.

"There aren't any suspects at the moment," Lauren told her.

"What about Mrs. Wagner?" Zoe asked. "Don't you think it's strange she wasn't there to help clean up?"

"We got there before Father Mike," Lauren pointed out, "and I'm sure he didn't do it."

"Good point." Zoe nodded. "What about Kyle?"

"Mitch said the waitress remembers him buying the burgers from Gary's Burger Diner," Lauren told her. "And he was carrying the burgers in that paper bag."

"But were there really burgers in there? Maybe he put some paper wads in there to make it look like he'd gone to get burgers." Zoe narrowed her eyes. "Did Mitch look inside the bag?"

"Of course he did," Lauren said. "Mitch knows what he's doing."

And he'd told her there were two burgers plus fries in that sack.

They finished getting the café ready for their first customer.

Today, Lauren had baked gingerbread cupcakes, as well as lemon poppyseed, and triple chocolate ganache.

"I hope these new Annie mugs sell." Zoe lined up the pottery she'd made, next to the register. The newest version featured Annie wearing a Santa hat, just like she'd worn for the play.

"I must be psychic, because I created these before Annie volunteered to be Mrs. Claus."

"You must be," Lauren teased. She crossed to the oak and glass entrance door and drew back the bolt. Before she could step back, a man barreled through.

"I know you did it." Kyle's face was flushed and he looked disheveled. "You killed my brother, and I'm going to prove it!"

CHAPTER 9

"What?" Lauren gasped.

"What?" Zoe's mouth fell open.

"Brrt??" Annie demanded from her basket.

"You two found him. That means you did it. Isn't it usually the killer who *pretends* to find the victim?" Kyle scowled at them.

"Not all the time." Zoe recovered. "We've found dead bodies before. And we didn't kill any of them!"

"Zoe!"

"Are you okay?" Ed poked his head out of the kitchen swinging door. He frowned at Kyle.

"Yeah, we're okay," Zoe told him.

He looked at them doubtfully. "Call me if you need help."

"We will," Lauren told him. "Thanks."

The kitchen door swung shut.

"I'm sorry about your brother," Lauren said to Kyle. "Truly." Although she hadn't cared for the little she'd known of

Jay, his death must be devastating for Kyle.

"But …" Lauren's sympathy seemed to mollify him a little. "… if you didn't kill him, who did?"

"I'm sure Mitch will find the killer," Lauren said. "If he was murdered, and it wasn't some kind of accident."

"A stab to the stomach doesn't seem like an accident." His eyebrows drew together, making him look forbidding.

"Did Mitch tell you that?" Zoe enquired.

"Of course. I'm the next of kin. And I saw the … blood."

"What about your mom?"

"She's next of kin too, but Jay and I lived together. Mom's in assisted living."

"Can we make you a latte or cappuccino?" Lauren indicated the coffee machine. "On the house."

"Or a mocha, espresso, Americano, hot chocolate, hot tea?" Zoe ran through their offerings.

"No, thanks." Kyle took a deep breath. "I'm sorry I blew up at you. Jay was a big part of my life. I don't know what I'm going to do without him."

He just stood there, sunk in thought.

"What about Father Mike?" He snapped his head up. "Do you think he knows anything?"

"Why would he?" Lauren was taken aback. "He wasn't there."

"Yeah, we were the only ones at the theater, apart from … Jay," Zoe told him. "Father Mike was at home because I called him after Mitch got there, and told him not to come because of what had happened."

"But was he really at home or did he just say he was at home?" Kyle narrowed his eyes. "Did you call him on his cell or landline?"

"Cell," Zoe admitted after a small pause.

"Father Mike wouldn't hurt a fly," Lauren protested. "He does a lot of good for the community."

"Yeah, everyone loves him." Zoe narrowed her own eyes as she stared at Kyle.

"I think you should talk to Mitch if you have any concerns," Lauren told him. "He's in charge of the case."

"That's right." Zoe nodded. "Mitch is doing the investigating." Lauren hoped only she heard her cousin mutter under her breath, "And if he doesn't catch the killer, we will."

***

"I can't believe his nerve," Zoe grumbled an hour later. "Honestly – do we look like killers?"

"Brrt." Annie tilted her head to the left as if she were shaking it no.

"Thanks, Annie." Zoe smiled down at her. "You always know what to say."

"And I don't?" Lauren asked wryly.

The confrontation with Kyle had shaken her. Unfortunately, it was a slow morning so far, without a lot of customers to focus on.

"I can't believe he tried to accuse Father Mike." Zoe frowned. "We'll have to tell him."

"Why?"

"To warn him. What if Kyle bangs on his door and accuses him of being a killer? Father Mike shouldn't have to deal with that."

"You're right. I'll call Mitch now and let him know."

"And I'll call Father Mike. I should have done it as soon as Kyle left but …" Zoe trailed off. "I was still processing it all."

"I hear you."

First, they'd stumbled upon Jay's body yesterday, and this morning his brother accused them of murder. It was a lot to deal with.

Lauren quickly told Mitch what had transpired while Zoe called Father Mike.

"Mitch is going to talk to Kyle," she told her cousin when they both finished their calls.

"Good." Zoe nodded. "Poor Father Mike sounded a little worried."

"Hopefully Mitch will catch up with Kyle before he decides to go over to the church."

"He'd better." Zoe sounded fierce.

The rest of the morning passed a lot more pleasantly. Mrs. Finch came in, as well as Martha.

"Now all we need is Hans to stop by."

"Don't forget Claire and little Molly," Lauren added.

"Brrt!" Annie's ears pricked up at the mention of three of her favorite customers.

To Annie's disappointment, Hans, Claire, and Molly didn't visit that morning.

"Mitch just texted me." Lauren showed Zoe the phone a little later. "He's warned Kyle not to approach Father Mike."

"Good." Zoe nodded, her pixie bangs bouncing against her forehead. "One less thing to worry about."

"What else is there?"

"Finding out who did it, of course." Zoe looked at her sideways. "You were here when Kyle roared in accusing us, weren't you?"

"I'm sure Mitch will find the murderer."

"But if he doesn't, we can start sleuthing." Excitement flickered across Zoe's face.

"Do you really think that's wise?"

Zoe was always the more enthusiastic of them when it came to sleuthing, or as Lauren tended to think of it, snooping, or *being nosy*.

120

"I don't want anyone else to accuse us of Jay's death. Do you?"

"No."

"And I'm sure Annie will want to help."

"Brrt?" Annie trotted toward them, her ears pricked and her green eyes shining with curiosity.

There were only a few customers in the café at the moment, and none of them sitting near the counter. Lauren thought that might change in thirty minutes, when the lunch rush usually started.

"Not here," Lauren admonished, flicking a warning glance at the seated customers.

"They won't be able to hear me," Zoe protested.

"You'll have to whisper." Lauren didn't want to take any chances.

"Annie," Zoe said in an exaggerated whisper as she bent down to the cat, "do you want to help us do some sleuthing and find out who killed Jay?"

"Brrt!" *Yes!*

***

Once again, Lauren was outvoted when it came to the matter of investigating a murder.

After the lunch rush, the café had emptied until it was only the three of them.

"I think we should give Mitch a chance to catch the killer first," she told Zoe and Annie.

Mitch was a good detective, and she didn't like interfering in his work. But she also didn't want their friends and customers, as well as Kyle, to think that she and Zoe had something to do with Jay's death.

"Oh, all right," Zoe grumbled. "I guess we can give him a couple of days."

"How generous." Lauren frowned at her cousin.

"Fine." Zoe's expression lifted a little. "You're right. Mitch does know what he's doing – I guess. It's just that I don't like a killer running around Gold Leaf Valley."

"Neither do I."

"Brrt!"

"So if we can't do some sleuthing right away, what can we do instead?"

"Get ready for Christmas?" Lauren suggested.

Their plans were still undecided. She hoped she and Mitch would spend the day together, but he wasn't sure if he would be on duty. And Zoe hadn't determined whether to visit her family in Sacramento over the holidays, or spend time with Chris – if he wasn't working.

"I've got your present." Zoe grinned. "Yours too, Annie."

"Brrt!" *Thank you.*

"And I've got both of yours," Lauren replied.

"We can always grab a turkey from the grocery store," Zoe said.

"If they haven't sold out by Christmas Eve," Lauren warned her.

Zoe shrugged. "We don't really know what we're doing though, do we? So let's just wing it."

Sometimes, winging it seemed to be Zoe's specialty.

"I know!" Zoe snapped her fingers. "We can go sofa shopping."

"Brrt?" Annie asked.

"Remember you suggested we buy a bigger sofa?" Zoe prompted Lauren. "And we haven't done anything about it."

"You're right." Lauren nodded. "But we've been busy."

"I know. But now might be the perfect time to go shopping!"

"The stores might be open later because it's Christmas time," Lauren mused.

"Exactly! In fact, I saw an ad last night on TV about a furniture store in Sacramento staying open in the evenings, *and* they deliver!"

"Are they having a sale?" Lauren asked hopefully. Price-matching sofas had slipped her mind, but Zoe was right. When Mitch and Chris came over to the cottage and they all watched a movie together, there wasn't enough room for all of them on the couch.

"Probably," Zoe said breezily. "I'll pay half the costs." She crossed to the tip jar next to the register and shook the coins onto the counter. There were a couple of bills stuffed in the glass jar as well.

"Ooh – fifteen dollars for me, and fifteen for Ed. Hey, what about instead of buying a sofa big enough for all four—" Zoe glanced down at Annie "—five of us, we buy a two-seater instead? It will be cheaper, and that way you, Mitch, and Annie could hang out on the couch we have now, and Chris and I could sit together on the other one."

"You mean you get to sit on the new sofa and I get to sit on the old one?" Lauren asked wryly.

"Yeah." The word *oops* flittered across her expression. "I mean—"

"It's okay. In fact, that might work better than the five us on one huge couch – if another sofa can fit in the living room."

"And we can all see the TV," Zoe added.

"Brrt!"

"Maybe we should take some measurements," Lauren suggested.

"And then we could go after work today!" Zoe's brown eyes lit up.

***

Since the rest of the afternoon had been quiet, Zoe persuaded Lauren to close fifteen minutes early. During the lull, Zoe had zipped back to the cottage, and measured the living room.

Now, as they stacked the chairs on the tables, Zoe told her what she'd discovered.

"If we move the current couch a little to the right, and the coffee table a little to the left, we should be able to squeeze in a new sofa."

"How much squeezing?" Lauren asked. The last thing she wanted to do was buy a sofa that wasn't going to fit in the space she had.

"Not much." Zoe flapped her hand in the air. "I'm sure it won't look a *total* squish. And you know what? I'm thinking we should buy another coffee table as well."

"What?"

"It makes sense," Zoe told her earnestly. "Two sofas and one coffee table in the middle – how is anyone going to reach from their seat and grab their mug or phone? You'd have to get up, take a step forward, and then pick up what you wanted. But if we had a coffee table in front of each couch ..."

"I hear you." Lauren nodded. She just hoped her checkbook did as well.

"I'll go halves on the coffee table as well," Zoe said brightly.

"Good." Lauren didn't want to know what her bank balance would look like after their shopping foray today.

They finished cleaning the café, then followed Annie down the private hallway that led to the cottage kitchen.

Lauren spooned some chicken in gravy into Annie's bowl, then sat down at the kitchen table for a second, before rising.

"You'd better show me your measurements," she told Zoe as she headed to the living room.

Zoe had already shoved the blue sofa to the right.

"See?" She indicated the little space she'd made. "I'm sure we can fit a two-seater in here."

"Can we find the same shade of blue?" Lauren asked. "I don't think we should get a total mishmash of colors happening in here."

"Of course not," Zoe agreed. "I know! We could get slip covers made for both couches if we can't find the right color tonight."

"That's a good idea. But how much is that going to cost? We're already buying a sofa and coffee table. And it's not as if either of us could make them."

Lauren had finally finished a two-tone tea cozy, but hadn't been game to use it in the café, as she didn't think it looked very good. After her struggle with changing colors – she now suspected that some of the color changes were falling apart – and following a pattern that had been marked 'easy' but had proven a little challenging for her beginner knitting skills – she had decided to take a short break.

Zoe was not known for her sewing, and neither was Lauren. In fact, Zoe usually shuddered when the word 'sewing' was mentioned.

"Maybe Mrs. Finch could make them," Zoe suggested hopefully.

"Do you really think Mrs. Finch is up to a big sewing project like that?" Lauren looked at her. Although their friend was experienced in handcrafts, she didn't think it fair to ask her to take on such a project.

"Probably not," Zoe admitted. "But maybe she knows someone who *could* do it, and would charge us a fair price."

"What about the clerk at the handmade shop?" Lauren suggested.

"Yes!" Zoe's eyes sparkled. "I'm sure she would have some recommendations."

Zoe talked about the potential slip covers during the drive to Sacramento. Annie had stayed behind in the cottage, saying hello to her friend Toby on a video play date.

"It's going to be so much fun choosing the right color. Something that goes with the décor we already have."

"And not too loud," Lauren said. "And Annie approved."

"Of course." Zoe nodded. "Not too pale either, so dirt doesn't show up so quickly."

"And easy to wash," Lauren added.

By the time they arrived at the furniture store, she was sure they'd be able to agree easily on the perfect sofa.

***

"This one!" Zoe zoomed to a plaid sofa with curved arms. "No, this one!" She raced over to a gold and cream striped sofa that looked like it should belong in a posh castle.

"That is beautiful." Lauren hurried after her cousin and admired the elegant creation.

The store was crowded with evening shoppers. The TV ads must have been very effective.

Lauren fingered the price tag and gasped. Three thousand dollars. No wonder it looked like it belonged to the aristocracy.

Zoe plopped down onto the satin upholstery and leaned back.

"Mmm." She closed her eyes and wiggled into the sofa.

"Zoe, get up. We can't afford it!"

Zoe slowly opened her eyes.

"We can't?" She frowned.

"No." Lauren showed her the price tag.

Zoe jumped up, shock flashing across her face. "Why didn't you tell me that before?"

Lauren just shook her head

"Hey, there." A man with gelled back hair came up to them. "Can I help you two find something?"

"Something like this." Zoe pointed to the gold and cream sofa she'd just tried out. "But much cheaper. Just as comfy, though."

"I can sign you two up for our super easy payment plan. Just one hundred down and minimum monthly payments. Spend the rest of your life in comfort." He flashed them a smile.

"No, thanks," they chorused.

The salesman eyed them, then heaved a sigh. "Then you'd better follow me."

They trailed after him as he led them through a maze of sectionals, coffee tables, and recliners, until he came to an area of the store that Lauren hadn't noticed before.

"Here you go." He pointed to plain colored couches and armchairs, interspersed with coffee tables. "Let me know if you find anything you like." He gazed past them, in the direction of the elegant sofa. "Gotta go and help that customer."

Lauren watched him dart back to the expensive section, where a well-to-do woman browsed.

"I'm sure these couches are just as good," Zoe said determinedly. She flopped down on a tan one. "Ow! There's a spring sticking up somewhere under the fabric." She jumped up and glared at the offending cushion seat.

"What about this one?" Lauren wandered over to a pale (but not too pale) pink two-seater. It looked quite nice and in a similar style to their blue couch. But if they were going to order slip covers, did it matter what color they chose?

She sat down carefully. Comfortable. Relaxing back into the seat, she reached over for the price tag. And blanched.

"Are you sure they're having a sale?" she asked Zoe.

"Well, I thought they might be," Zoe admitted. She sank down next to Lauren. "This feels nice." She wiggled. "Yeah."

"The price isn't. It costs four hundred dollars!"

"I'm paying half, remember? And it's not three thousand."

"But we still have to buy a coffee table."

"Now we've decided on this one, we can choose a coffee table together." Zoe jumped up.

"Do you think this sofa will fit in the living room?" Lauren dug out the tape measure from her purse. "Help me?"

"Okay." Zoe held one end of the tape and Lauren the other as they measured the back of the sofa. "Yes, it will totally—" she suddenly dropped the measure, ran around the sofa, and disappeared from view. "Hide!"

"What?" Lauren whirled around but didn't see anyone they knew. "Zoe?"

"Quick!" Zoe whispered urgently.

Lauren obeyed, dropping down on the carpet next to her, the couch shielding them.

"What is going on?"

"Mrs. Wagner. Over there."

"Where?" Lauren half rose.

"No! She'll see us!" Zoe tugged her back down.

"So?" Lauren crinkled her brow.

"What is she doing here? I just saw her talking with a salesman. And not in this

133

cheap section. In a more expensive section."

"You think this furniture is cheap?" Lauren shook her head, then focused on the rest of Zoe's words. "How could she see us if she's not close by?"

"Because she has eyes like an eagle," Zoe muttered. "She was always noticing something wrong with the costumes for the play. I bet if she turned her head slightly, she would have seen us."

"And that's bad because …?"

"Because she has no money! So what is she doing in a furniture store?"

"Maybe she's with a friend," Lauren suggested.

"Nope. There was no one with her."

"Maybe she's window shopping."

"Then why come inside?"

"Maybe she wants to sign up for their payment plan." Lauren was running out of ideas.

"And pay tons of interest?"

"We don't know for sure there'll be a ton of interest." Lauren tried to be fair. "But I thought it best to say no and only buy what we could afford – or what we thought we could afford."

"Me too." Zoe grinned. Then sobered. "So what is Mrs. Wagner doing here?"

"Why don't we ask her?"

"What if she murdered Jay?"

"Do you really think she could have done such a thing?" Lauren stared at her.

"Someone had to. And we know she was mad at him because he destroyed her expensive, rare, rose bush."

"True."

"And she had to save up for it."

"Also true."

"And she hasn't been able to find a replacement."

"Triple true. But what has being in this store got to do with killing Jay?" Lauren frowned. "It's not as if Jay had a wad of cash on him, she killed him, and stole his money."

"Isn't it?"

"I think Mitch would have told me – us – if there had been a large sum of money missing from Jay's wallet. Surely Kyle would have known if there had been?"

"I guess you're right," Zoe replied after a moment. "And Jay always seemed to be short of cash. Remember at dress rehearsal when he told Kyle he couldn't pay for his share of the groceries? He was going to ask his mom for a loan."

"I know." Lauren had thought it seemed a little immature since he had a job, although she didn't know what he did.

"But if Mrs. Wagner has no money, then why is she shopping for furniture?" Zoe half rose and peered above the back of the sofa. "I can't see her."

"Good." She was tired of crouching down. Maybe Mrs. Wagner hadn't spotted them, but what about the people browsing behind them? Had they even noticed their antics? Lauren was glad a sales clerk hadn't demanded to know what they were doing.

She stood and turned around. No one giggling or staring at her sideways. Good.

"Now we have to look for coffee tables. Come on!"

***

They didn't see Mrs. Wagner again. After Zoe haggled a little with the same hair-gelled salesman, they bought a simple oak coffee table, and the pink sofa

136

they'd agreed on. They were promised delivery before Christmas Eve.

"Now all we have to do is decide on a color for the slip covers," Zoe declared as they drove home.

"I think Annie will like the sofa before we get it covered, anyway," Lauren said. "She likes pink."

"Just like us." Zoe grinned. "Hey! We could just order pink covers and recover the old blue sofa with them. The new couch won't need covering."

"Good idea." Lauren nodded. They'd had the blue couch for a while and it was starting to look a *little* shabby. And two pink sofas would look good together.

CHAPTER 10

"We ordered a pretty pink sofa," Lauren told Annie that night. "And a coffee table."

"And we're going to cover this blue couch with a pink cover," Zoe added. The three of them sat on that piece of furniture as they watched a show about making your own clothes.

"It's a shame they're not making slip covers in this episode," Lauren teased as the girl on the screen operated her sewing machine like a racing car driver.

"I wish I could sew like that." Zoe sounded wistful instead of her usual shuddery side-eyes when someone mentioned sewing. "Just imagine the outfits I could create for myself. And for you too, Lauren," she added.

"Brrt?" Annie asked.

"Of course I would make you a cute little something," Zoe told her. "But I can't sew."

"Me neither," Lauren agreed ruefully. She yawned. "I'm going to bed."

"I might as well, too." Zoe glanced at her phone. "Chris is working tonight but he thinks he'll be off Christmas Day, so I was thinking we could spend the day together."

"That's great." Lauren smiled.

"Brrt!"

They turned off the TV and headed to their bedrooms. Annie curled up in Lauren's bed, while Lauren tossed and turned for a while. Zoe had a point – why had Mrs. Wagner been in the furniture store that evening? Was her visit totally innocent … or totally sinister?

***

The next morning, Zoe hummed a Christmas tune as she arranged her pottery mugs on the counter.

"I think today is the day we start using my cups for customers," she announced to Lauren and Annie.

"You're right," Lauren agreed, feeling a little guilty that they hadn't done that already. It had seemed such a great idea a couple of months ago when Zoe had come up with the notion, but between creating new cupcake creations and spending time with Annie and their respective boyfriends, as well as Zoe making enough mugs to serve all their customers if the café was super busy, well …

"I've got plenty of inventory now." Zoe grinned. "I think we should use the mugs featuring Annie's show girl pose, and her new Christmas one."

"Brrt!" Annie agreed, her green eyes shining as she looked up at the counter where the white mugs were arrayed in a neat line.

"These are for the customers, in case they want to buy one to take home," Zoe told her. "The mugs they'll use in the café are behind the counter, next to the espresso machine."

"See?" Lauren stood behind the counter and picked up a cup, showing Annie the portrait of herself wearing a blue winner's sash. Zoe had been inspired by Annie's participation in a local cat show a couple of months ago.

"And this is my – our – new Christmas design." Zoe hefted a mug that showed Annie wearing a Santa hat. She'd drawn the portraits of the Norwegian Forest Cat herself, and had included the name of the café.

"Brrt." *Thank you.* Annie looked pleased.

Since Zoe had started making pottery mugs, a lot of their customers had bought them. It had been Zoe's most successful hobby to date, and Lauren wondered if she would stick with it, instead of being attracted to another handcraft.

"Now all we need are some customers," Lauren commented.

A few minutes after they opened, Hans walked in.

"Brrt!" Annie ran to greet him.

"Hello, *Liebchen.*" He bent stiffly to greet Annie. "How are you today?"

"Brrt!" *I'm good!*

"Hi, Hans," Lauren called.

"Hello, Lauren, and Zoe." His faded blue eyes twinkled as he smiled at them.

"What can we get you?" Zoe asked.

"I think I'll try one of Ed's Danishes today," he told them.

"Apricot Danish or honeyed walnut?" Lauren queried.

"Apricot, please," he replied. "And a cappuccino."

"We'll bring it over," Lauren promised as Annie slowly led him to a four-seater table near the counter.

"Ta-daa!" A few minutes later, Zoe carried a tray over to the table. "You are the first to use my pottery mugs as a customer," she told him proudly.

"Ach, *Liebchen,* you are wearing the Santa Claus hat from the play." Hans admired the pottery portrait of Annie.

"Brrt!" *Yes!*

"This is very fine, Zoe," Hans told her, nodding. "You are a good potter."

"Thanks." Zoe beamed. "I don't think these mugs have any mistakes, either. My first attempts months ago had a bulge near the handle, but now I think they look pretty good."

"They do," Lauren told her, joining them. "And your artwork is great, too."

"Thanks." Zoe's beam widened. "Your latte art is amazing," she added. "Lauren made a swan on top of your micro foam," she told Hans.

"Ach, yes, I see." Hans smiled at them, so looking like Santa Claus at that moment that Lauren had to blink. The only thing missing was a bigger stomach.

"What are you doing for Christmas?" Lauren asked.

"I am visiting my daughter in Sacramento."

"That's great." Zoe grinned.

"But I must ask you – is it true that you found Jay at the theater? And he was … dead?" he asked delicately.

"Yes." Lauren nodded.

"We were there to help Father Mike clean up after the performance," Zoe added.

"It is no good that you two are always finding dead bodies," he said gravely. "I am glad you are alright."

"So are we," Lauren said fervently.

"Kyle came in yesterday and accused us of killing his brother," Zoe told him indignantly. "As if we would do such a thing!"

"Kyle?" Hans frowned. "Is that the brother of Jay – the man you found?"

"Yes," Lauren replied.

"But I saw him go into the theater with his brother."

"When was that?" Zoe pounced.

"On Monday afternoon. I am walking past and I see the two of them go toward the back stage entrance."

"Hmm." Zoe tapped her cheek. "Didn't Kyle say he was out getting burgers and was going to join Jay at the theater? He didn't mention arriving there with Jay and then leaving to get burgers."

"That's right." Lauren chewed her lip.

"That is not *gut*." Hans shook his head. "Brrp." *No*.

"You must be very careful," Hans told them.

"We will." Lauren fished out her phone from the pocket of her festive red and white apron. "Do you mind if I call Mitch and tell him this? He might want to ask you some questions."

"Of course." Hans dug his fork into the glistening, golden, apricot Danish, the tender, flaky, pastry leaves clinging to the tines. "If I had known it was important, I would have contacted him myself as soon as I heard at the senior center of Jay's death."

Lauren called Mitch and briefly told him what Hans had just told her.

"He said he'll come over right away and talk to you about what you saw."

"That is fine." Hans nodded.

Lauren and Zoe left Hans to enjoy his visit with Annie.

"Ha! I knew there was something about those two brothers," Zoe said as they headed back to the counter. "Although, I thought Jay was a bit sketchy and Kyle seemed mostly okay."

"Maybe there's a logical explanation," Lauren suggested.

"The only logical thing is Kyle lied. And I'm going to find out why!"

***

Mitch arrived at the café a few minutes later. Luckily, there weren't any other customers, so he could have some privacy questioning Hans, with Annie 'supervising'.

Lauren brought over her boyfriend a latte, which he received with a grateful look.

"I wonder what Hans is saying to him." Zoe peered over at them.

"I'm sure we'll find out soon," Lauren said, hoping her prediction was true.

"I don't think he noticed you gave him one of my – Annie's – mugs." Zoe furrowed her brow.

"I'm sure he will if you give him a chance."

Lauren watched Mitch write down something in his notebook.

"You can grill him later, anyway," Zoe told her. "When you two are alone."

"You know I don't like to interfere in Mitch's work."

"Luckily I don't have that problem." Zoe grinned.

"Zoe!"

After Mitch finished speaking with Hans, he came over to the counter.

"Thanks for calling me," he told Lauren. "Hans has given me some valuable information."

"Good," Lauren murmured.

"What did he say?" Zoe asked.

"What I'm sure he already told both of you." His mouth quirked slightly.

Zoe looked like she wasn't quite convinced.

After making plans to have dinner with him that night, Lauren watched him go.

"So what are you two up to this evening?" Zoe wanted to know. She'd headed down to the other end of the counter to give them some privacy – or the illusion of it.

Lauren told her of their dinner plans.

"Chris is working again tonight." She wrinkled her nose.

"I'm sorry," Lauren sympathized.

"But we did have a great time hiking on Sunday." Zoe brightened. "When both guys are free, maybe we can all go on a double date."

"That would be fun." Lauren smiled. They'd already gone on a few doubles, and they had worked out well.

"Hey!" Zoe snapped her fingers. "Instead of us organizing it this time, maybe the guys could. Since they're roomies at the moment."

"Good idea."

"I'll text Chris." Zoe whipped out her phone from her jeans' pocket.

***

That evening, Lauren sat across a small table from Mitch at the bistro on the outskirts of Gold Leaf Valley. The interior was rustic but welcoming.

"I'll have to re-interview Kyle," Mitch told her as they waited for their entrees. "At the moment, his account doesn't quite tally with Hans'."

"Mmm." Lauren was certain Hans was trustworthy. He might be in his sixties, but his brain was sharp.

However, she didn't know much about Kyle.

Mitch captured her hand.

"So, I was thinking," he said tenderly, "I could stay over at the cottage Saturday night. I'm not on duty, and we could go out to dinner first."

Lauren stared at him, her heart suddenly beating fast.

They'd previously arranged a romantic weekend away together – their first – which hadn't turned out as expected, due to a murder taking place. Although they'd spoken about it recently, between their work and now Chris temporarily moving in with Mitch, they hadn't actually taken their relationship to the next level.

"Yes."

"Yes?" He smiled.

"Yes." She nodded, sure that now was the right time. They'd taken things slowly – she was positive a lot of people these days would have said far too slowly – but now she didn't have any doubts that this was what she wanted to do, and where she wanted the relationship to go.

"I think Chris is off on Saturday."

"Does Zoe know?" she asked.

"She will in a sec."

He dug his phone out of his jacket and texted.

"I asked Chris to organize something with Zoe on Saturday night. He was going to, anyway."

"Zoe will be pleased."

"Yeah." The warm desire in his eyes plainly told her he was pleased as well.

"We could always go to your place," she teased.

"No." He shook his head. "Your cottage is you – soft and friendly and – just you."

"Whereas your place is …?" She was curious to hear his answer.

"A bit of a mess." His tone was honest. "It's got the basics, and I try to keep it tidy, but since Chris moved in, I haven't straightened up as much as I should."

"Okay," she murmured, her thoughts already racing to Saturday. Where would they go to dinner? What should she wear? What should she wear underneath? Something soft and inviting?

CHAPTER 11

The next morning, Lauren was still deciding what to wear for her date with Mitch.

"What about your plum wrap dress?" Zoe suggested as she unstacked the chairs in the café. "Or your teal one?"

"Brrt," Annie agreed as she sat in her pink bed, watching them get the space ready.

"Mitch has seen those tons of times," Lauren said. They were two of her favorite 'date night' outfits.

"And he likes them, doesn't he?"

"Yes," Lauren admitted.

"But that doesn't mean you can't wear something special underneath." Zoe winked.

Lauren blushed. She actually had something "special" that she'd bought for their romantic weekend away that had turned out not to be so romantic after all. And since she hadn't worn it since then, it was practically new.

"I think I've got it covered," she told her cousin.

"Or uncovered." Zoe giggled.

Lauren flapped a hand at her and hurried into the kitchen to check on the cupcakes.

"Hi, Ed," she greeted her pastry chef.

"Hi," he grunted, briefly looking up from his satiny dough.

The gingerbread cupcakes were now cool enough to frost. Lauren grabbed the bowl from the fridge and concentrated on making each swirl of frosting a work of art – so she wouldn't have to think about Saturday night.

Of course she wanted Mitch to stay over. It was time. But she couldn't help feeling a mixture of anticipation and nervousness.

Before she knew it, all the cakes were iced and looked so tempting she had to stop herself from eating one – right now.

"I'll take these outside," she told Ed, who didn't even grunt this time, so engrossed in cutting out pinwheels of his famous pastry.

"Ms. Tobin is out there already," Zoe told her as she carried the tray of goodies into the café. "I'm going to let her in."

"Okay." Lauren carefully placed the treats inside the glass case. She'd already finished frosting the vanillas, and triple chocolate ganache cupcakes.

"Hello, girls." Ms. Tobin swept in and strode to the counter. "Oh, you do have them!" She picked up a Christmas mug featuring Annie wearing a Santa hat.

"They're my new creation," Zoe told her as she zoomed behind the counter. "Only fifteen dollars."

"I must have one." Ms. Tobin pulled her wallet out of her handbag.

"Brrt?" Annie trotted to greet her.

"This is the only mug of yours I don't have, Annie," she told the cat. "I've bought all your others, including your showgirl creation."

"Thanks, Ms. Tobin." Zoe grinned as she rang up the sale.

"My friend at the senior center told me about them yesterday," Ms. Tobin continued. "I must say, Zoe, your pottery skills are quite good now."

Zoe's grin widened.

"And now I will have my usual large latte and one of your gingerbread cupcakes."

"Coming right up," Lauren promised.

Annie led her to a table and perched on the opposite chair.

"I think Ms. Tobin is one of my biggest fans when it comes to these mugs," Zoe said.

"I think you're right," Lauren agreed.

They quickly filled the order and brought it over.

"Thank you." Ms. Tobin nodded as she surveyed the swan on top of the latte. "Very good latte art, Lauren."

"I'm glad you like it." Lauren smiled.

"I was just telling Annie I hope she has a wonderful Christmas. Are you going to be closed over the holidays?"

Lauren and Zoe looked at each other.

"Umm ... we haven't really discussed it."

"Yeah." Zoe nodded.

"We won't be open on Christmas Day, but I'm not sure what our plans are yet."

"Of course," Ms. Tobin replied.

"Are you doing something for Christmas?" Zoe asked her.

"I'm spending the day with my friend." Ms. Tobin smiled slightly. "We will share the cooking – and the cleaning up. She makes a wonderful apple and walnut stuffing, and I think I make a very nice sweet potato dish, so it should work out well."

"That's good," Lauren said, glad that Ms. Tobin wasn't going to spend the day alone – unless that was what she wanted to do.

"That's an amazing brooch." Zoe gestured to the dainty red stones on the lapel of Ms. Tobin's fawn sweater, depicting a poinsettia.

"Thank you." Ms. Tobin fingered it. "I thought it rather pretty when I was shopping recently, so decided to treat myself."

After a moment, they left her to enjoy her time with Annie, and headed back to the counter.

"It's craft club tomorrow," Zoe said.

"And I'm not doing anything crafty." Lauren felt guilty.

"We can talk about your hot date with Mitch instead." Zoe winked.

Lauren shook her head. "What are you going to do while I'm having dinner with Mitch?"

"Doing something with Chris," Zoe said breezily. "I get to choose."

"Again?"

"He knows I like choosing. And sometimes I let him choose."

"That's kind of you." Lauren suppressed a smile.

"Isn't it?" Zoe giggled. "Don't worry, I won't cramp your style Saturday night."

"Thanks."

"I'll just creep into the house after my date with Chris, as quiet as a mouse. You won't even hear me. Or maybe I'll stay over at his place."

"You mean Mitch's place."

"It's both their place at the moment," Zoe informed her. "And I might not stay there, because it sounds a bit messy. Chris is crashing on the sofa."

"That doesn't sound comfortable."

"Nope."

***

156

The rest of the day sped by. Lauren and Zoe started cleaning up as soon as they bolted the door shut.

Lauren had just plugged in the vacuum when she heard a knock on the entrance door.

"Who's that?" Zoe looked over from stacking the last chair.

Lauren hurried toward the door, then stopped halfway.

"It's Kyle."

"What's he doing here?" Zoe marched over to the door and peered through the glass panel. "We're not open," she called out.

"Need coffee." He called back, and tapped his watch with a frown.

Lauren glanced at her practical white wristwatch. It was one minute after five. They had closed up a few minutes early because there hadn't been any customers.

"What should we do?" Zoe asked.

If it had been one of their regulars, she would have gladly let them in. But it was Kyle …

"Maybe I can grill him while you make him coffee," Zoe suggested, pulling back the bolt.

"Zoe …" But it was too late. Kyle strode into the café.

"Thanks," he told them.

"What can we get you?" Lauren gestured at the glass case. "I'm afraid all the cupcakes and pastries have sold out."

"Not a problem. I only wanted a latte. I had a tough day at work."

"I'm sorry," Lauren said awkwardly.

"Yeah, ordinarily I would have asked for some more time off, but since I'm new there – Jay was, too – I need the income."

"What do you do?" Zoe asked.

"We – I – work at that new warehouse outside town. I'm one of the supervisors and Jay is – was – a packer there."

"I'll make you that latte." She hadn't turned off the machine yet.

"Did Mitch talk to you about the eyewitness who saw you enter the theater on Monday?" Zoe jumped in, ignoring Lauren's warning frown.

"Yeah." He laughed shortly. "The guy was totally mistaken. I only went into the theater after I grabbed the burgers for me and Jay." He swallowed hard. "Monday was our day off. We thought we'd do something good for the community, show we meant well, but instead …" His voice broke.

"Sorry," Lauren murmured, the espresso machine growling as it ground the coffee beans.

"Who do you think killed your brother?" Zoe persisted.

"I don't know." He shrugged. "We haven't lived here long, so I don't think Jay made any enemies – not that I know of, anyway."

"Where are you from?" Zoe continued.

"LA." His eyes narrowed. "What is this, an interrogation?"

"Not really," Zoe replied, but her tone implied otherwise.

"I could ask you two more questions about why you were backstage at the theater so early, but I believed you when you said you didn't kill my brother," Kyle told them. "It works both ways, you know."

"How's your mom doing?" Lauren asked as she created a tulip on top of the foam.

"She's holding up well," he told them. "Although it's a shock for her because she didn't expect to outlive her kids."

"I can imagine," Lauren murmured. "Here you go." She handed him the latte in a to-go cup.

"Thanks." He gave her some cash and put fifty cents into the tip jar. "I definitely need this today." He took a sip, keeping the lid in place, so he didn't even see the artwork Lauren had crafted.

"We have to clean up now." Zoe moved toward the entrance door.

"Oh – right." He nodded, and strode out of the door she held open for him.

Zoe shot the bolt as soon as he stepped outside.

"Brrt?" Annie called from her cat bed. She'd stayed there the whole time. Was she tired from her hostess duties, or did she not care for Kyle?

"I don't think we should have let him in," Zoe mused, "although I did try to grill him."

"I noticed," Lauren said dryly. She'd felt uncomfortable during the whole encounter.

"Brrt?" Annie called again

"What is it?" Lauren walked over to the silver-gray tabby.

"Brrt!" Annie flipped up the corner of her pink cushion. A glint of red sparkled in the overhead light.

Lauren reached in and picked up the object.

"What's Annie got there?" Zoe zoomed over to them.

"It's Ms. Tobin's poinsettia brooch." Lauren turned it over in her hand. The dainty red stones formed the petals of the festive flower.

"What's it doing in Annie's basket?" Zoe scrunched her nose.

"Maybe it fell off when Ms. Tobin was here earlier," Lauren suggested

"Brrt," Annie agreed.

"Thank you for looking after it, Annie." Lauren smiled at her fur baby. "I'll keep this in a safe place for Ms. Tobin."

"Brrp."

"Let's call Ms. Tobin and let her know." Zoe pulled out her phone from her jeans' pocket. "Remember when she wanted to order some extra cupcakes and gave us her number?"

"Good idea." Lauren watched her cousin's fingers fly on the phone.

Zoe spoke briefly with Ms. Tobin. "She's coming over right away." She stuck the device back into her pocket. "She didn't even notice it had fallen off her sweater."

"I'm sure she'll be pleased to find out you were minding it for her," Lauren told Annie.

"Brrt!"

Ten minutes later, they let Ms. Tobin into the café.

"Here you are." Lauren handed her the brooch.

"Brrt!" Annie trotted to greet her.

"Thank you, Annie, dear." Ms. Tobin looked harried. "I'm so glad you found it." She studied the back of the ornament. "I've noticed before this silver pin is a little flimsy. That must be why it fell off." She re-attached the brooch to her sweater. "There."

"It looks lovely," Lauren complimented.

"Thank you, Lauren." Ms. Tobin smiled at her. She looked around the café, spotting the chairs stacked on the tables. "I must let you get on with things."

They waved goodbye to Ms. Tobin as she left.

"Well, that's one mystery solved," Zoe declared as she resumed stacking the chairs.

"And one we didn't even know needed solving." Lauren smiled.

"Now we just have to find out who killed Jay!"

CHAPTER 12

"I wonder what Mrs. Finch is doing for Christmas," Zoe mused the next evening as they drove to their friend's house. The evening was chilly, damp – and dark.

"I hope she won't be on her own," Lauren said.

"She can always spend Christmas with us," Zoe suggested.

"Good idea." It was the perfect solution – if Mrs. Finch didn't already have plans.

Lauren pulled up outside the sweet Victorian cottage. The porch lamp glowed in the night.

She lifted Annie out of the backseat, checking the buckles on her harness were secure.

"Brrt." Annie led the way to the front door.

"Hello, dears." Mrs. Finch greeted them before they even had a chance to knock. "I heard your car and saw your headlights."

"Hi, Mrs. Finch." Zoe beamed at her.

"Come in, come in." The elderly lady led the way down the lilac hall to the living room, decorated in shades of fawn and beige.

"Now, what crafts are we going to explore tonight?" she asked as she carefully sat down in an armchair.

"I've just finished the latest batch of Annie's mugs." Zoe pulled a brightly wrapped gift out of her shopping bag and handed it to Mrs. Finch.

"This is for you. From me and Annie. And Lauren."

"Brrt!" Annie sat next to Lauren on the sofa, watching Mrs. Finch with wide green eyes.

"How lovely!" Mrs. Finch's hands wobbled slightly as she unwrapped the present. She gazed at the portrait of Annie wearing a Santa hat. "Annie, it looks just like you, dear." She beamed.

"Brrt!" *Thank you.*

"What are you doing for the holidays?" Lauren asked, giving Zoe a sideways glance. A small plastic tree decorated with a few silver baubles stood in the corner of the room.

"Oh, girls, I just found out today. My son and his wife are coming to spend Christmas here." Mrs. Finch's face was wreathed in smiles.

"That's wonderful." Lauren was glad their friend would spend time with her family.

"Awesome!"

"Now, Lauren, how is your knitting going?"

"It's not," Lauren said gloomily.

"Wait until you see what Santa is bringing you." Zoe winked at her.

"Wool?" Lauren asked half hopefully and half unhopefully.

"You've done very well since you took up knitting," Mrs. Finch encouraged her. "You've stuck with it and you've made two scarves and hats, and a tea cozy."

"I think the tea cozy is where I came *unstuck.*" Lauren wrinkled her nose. "It was a lot harder to make than I thought, and I don't think it's good enough to use in the café."

"If you take a break you might want to return to knitting at a later point," Mrs. Finch encouraged.

"Yeah, like on Christmas Day." Zoe giggled.

Lauren glanced at her. What was her cousin up to?

Mrs. Finch told them more about her son's visit, and then Lauren and Zoe went to the kitchen to make them all a latte.

"We must ask her about Jay and Kyle's mom," Zoe muttered as Lauren dropped a capsule into the coffee machine. "Maybe Mrs. Finch knows something."

"True," Lauren agreed, as the machine growled and hummed, pouring out a thin stream of espresso.

After Lauren made the coffee, they returned to the living room. Annie was now perched on the arm of Mrs. Finch's chair.

"Thank you, girls." Mrs. Finch beamed at them as Lauren handed her a latte. "What shall we talk about now?"

"Jay getting murdered." Zoe jumped in. "I think we should find out who did it."

"And I think we should let Mitch catch the killer," Lauren commented.

"Do you know their mom?" Zoe asked.

"No." Mrs. Finch shook her head. "I heard she's in assisted living, but I'm afraid I haven't met her."

"That's too bad." Zoe frowned.

"I don't think she's very well," Mrs. Finch said thoughtfully. "I can't remember who told me that, though."

"Maybe Martha knows something," Zoe suggested. "We can ask her next time she's in the café."

"Brrt!" *Yes!*

"I hope you three will be careful," Mrs. Finch fretted.

"We will," Lauren told her.

They moved on to more pleasant topics, Zoe leaving the subject of Lauren's date with Mitch until last.

Thankfully, she didn't embarrass Lauren too much, just telling Mrs. Finch with a wink that Lauren had a big date with Mitch the following night.

"I think he is a very nice young man," Mrs. Finch told her. "Although, I did not like him when he first came to town and investigated my neighbor Steve's death. But he was doing his job and I think he might have mellowed a little since he's met you, Lauren."

"Ohh." Lauren didn't know what to say but she could feel her cheeks heat up at the compliment.

They said goodbye to Mrs. Finch and walked out to the car.

"Now we – I – have another mystery to solve," Zoe declared with a giggle as she buckled her seatbelt. "Where am I going to sleep tomorrow night?"

***

"I'm taking Chris to meet my parents," Zoe told her the next morning over breakfast.

Lauren's spoonful of granola paused halfway to her mouth.

"Brrt?" *You are*? Annie asked as she sat next to Lauren at the table.

"When?"

"Tonight." Zoe nodded. "So that means you can have the house to yourself – with Mitch. And Annie, of course. Chris and I will have dinner with Mom and Dad."

"What does Chris think about it?" Lauren asked, curious.

169

"He doesn't know yet." Zoe waved a hand airily. "But he did say I could choose what we did tonight."

"You haven't met his parents yet – have you?" Lauren peered at her cousin. They told each other pretty much everything, but this announcement was a little surprising.

"No," Zoe admitted. "Although we have talked about it – a bit. Anyway, this is the perfect solution for tonight. Chris and I could even stay overnight at my parents if we don't feel like driving all way back here. And I can stay over at his – and Mitch's – apartment if we do get back here late."

"If you're sure," Lauren said a little dubiously. It would be nice to have the place to herself – and Mitch, but she didn't want her cousin to feel displaced.

"I am." Zoe pulled out her phone from her jacket pocket. "I'll text Chris right now and tell him I've made our plans for the night."

***

That evening, butterflies flitted in Lauren's stomach. Zoe had already gone to pick up Chris, a giggle on her lips as she left. Lauren hoped Chris was ready to meet Zoe's parents, and her cousin's surprise wouldn't backfire.

Now it was her turn to get ready for her date with Mitch.

"Brrt?" Annie asked as she jumped up on the bed, effortlessly elegant.

"I'm going to wear my plum wrap dress. Mitch and I are going out to dinner, then coming back here." Lauren pulled the outfit out of the closet.

She felt comfortable in it – and attractive. Mitch's eyes always warmed when he saw her wear it.

"Mitch is going to stay over tonight." Lauren pointed at the bed. "In here with me."

"Brrt?" Annie's eyes rounded.

"Yes." Lauren nodded, hoping Annie wouldn't be upset about the sleeping arrangements for the night. "So, I was thinking, you could sleep on the sofa in the living room?"

"Brrt?" Annie's eyes grew even wider.

"It's just for one night," Lauren said hastily. Although, if things went well like she hoped they would, it might be more.

"Brrp." Annie's lower lip jutted out.

"Mitch and I are going to be doing … girlfriend-boyfriend things." She hoped. Glad there weren't any witnesses right now as she tried to delicately explain adult relationships to her fur baby, she continued, "I don't think you should be in here while we're … together like that."

"Brrp." Lauren didn't think it was possible for Annie's lower lip to pout any further.

"You like Mitch, don't you?" Lauren asked as she slipped on the dress. It had taken Annie a little while to warm up to Mitch, but now she seemed to accept him readily as Lauren's boyfriend.

"Brrp," Annie replied.

Lauren told herself it meant *Yes*.

"He might be over here a little more often," she told her fur baby. "Because he likes me – us."

Mitch hadn't had any experience with cats when she'd first met him, and he'd also taken time to get used to Annie, but now both of them seemed to like each other.

Annie turned around in a circle on the bed, appearing to think it over. Then she settled down on the peach bedspread, as if she was not going to move anytime soon.

"Okay." Lauren kissed the top of her head, the fur velvety soft. She hadn't had a boyfriend for a while before she'd met Mitch – in fact, she didn't think she'd had overnight company since Annie had come into her life. Mitch staying tonight might be a bit of an adjustment for Annie – but it might also be one for Lauren as well.

By the time Mitch arrived, Lauren was ready. Annie was asleep on the bed, not even stirring when the doorbell sounded.

"Hi." He smiled at her, looking extra handsome in his outfit of charcoal slacks and navy dress shirt, the colors complimenting his short dark hair and brown eyes.

"Hi," she said breathlessly.

"Where's Annie?" He looked past her.

"Having a snooze." Maybe she would wait until later to tell him about Annie's reaction to their plans for the night.

"I'll say hi to her when we get back." He smiled.

She nodded, locking the door behind her as they headed toward his car.

***

Lauren found it hard to concentrate on conversation during dinner at the Italian restaurant at Zeke's Ridge, a small town not too far away.

Mitch ordered steak with mushrooms, while she tried ratatouille.

The memory of their thwarted romantic weekend away flashed through her mind. At least there wouldn't be a horrible surprise when they returned to the cottage – she hoped. Annie had always been so well-behaved – even if she wasn't entirely happy about tonight, Lauren was sure she wouldn't "act out" and claw a pillow, or the sweater Lauren just remembered she'd left lying on the bed.

"What's Zoe up to tonight?" Mitch asked as they waited for their dessert of tiramisu.

"Taking Chris to meet her parents." Lauren couldn't hide a little smile.

"Really?" Surprise flickered across his face.

"Yes."

"I hope it goes well," he replied. "Chris definitely has feelings for her."

"And Zoe definitely has feelings for him."

"Good." He captured her hand, giving her all his attention.

After dinner they drove back to the cottage. Lauren opened the front door with trepidation, wondering if Annie would be standing in the hallway, looking at her reproachfully, but the house was silent.

She flicked on the light.

No Annie.

"Where is she?" Mitch asked.

Now was the time to tell him.

"I don't think she …" her voice trailed off as they entered the living room. Her fur baby was curled up on the sofa, nestled in Lauren's sweater – the one she'd left on the bed.

"Ohhh." Was this Annie's way of telling her she was okay with Mitch spending the night?

"Let's not disturb her," Mitch whispered, his arm around Lauren's shoulder.

"No."

***

Later, Lauren wondered why she had been nervous. It had been wonderful – and definitely worth the wait. She'd shut the bedroom door as a precaution, but there had been no four-footed scratching, demanding to be let in.

She snuggled in Mitch's arms, drifting off to sleep.

***

"Hey." A soft male voice near her ear.

"Mmm?" Lauren burrowed under the covers.

"I think someone wants to see you." Mitch sounded amused.

Lauren sat up, blinking.

Mitch was right next to her – in bed.

Scratch, scratch, on the closed bedroom door. *Scratch, scratch.*

"Ohhh." She looked at him, nonplussed. "Annie usually sleeps with me."

"I guessed," he said wryly. "It's okay. Why don't I make us some coffee and give you two some time together?"

Her heart filled with love at his understanding.

"Thanks," she replied softly.

He kissed her tenderly on the lips.

Mitch left for the kitchen, wearing his clothes from last night.

"Brrt!" Annie rushed into the room and jumped onto the bed, her eyes wide and curious. "Brrt!"

"Thank you for last night." Lauren stroked the silver-gray tabby. "I love you so much, and I always will. You know that, don't you?"

"Brrt." *Yes.*

"You'll always be my fur baby."

"Brrt!" *Good!*

Mitch came back into the bedroom, carrying two mugs.

"These lattes won't be as good as yours, but they should be drinkable." He set the mugs down, smiling at Annie. "Good morning, Annie."

"Brrt." She looked at him for a second, then nestled into Lauren's arms again. After a moment, she peeked out at him. "Brrt?"

"I think she might be inviting you to pet her," Lauren said.

"Okay." Mitch gently stroked Annie's shoulder. "I'll take good care of your mom," he told her. "And you too, if you'll let me."

Lauren's eyes grew misty. She had definitely made the right decision letting Mitch into her – and Annie's – life.

CHAPTER 13

Zoe and Chris arrived at the cottage mid-morning.

"Is it safe to come in?" Zoe called out as she exaggeratedly tiptoed into the kitchen.

"Yes." Lauren smiled as she greeted her cousin.

"Brrt!"

"Hi, Annie." Chris bent down to the feline. "How are you?"

"Brrt." *Good.*

"So, did you meet Zoe's parents?" Lauren teased.

"Yes," Chris replied.

"Did you?" Mitch entered the kitchen, his lips quirking.

"Mom and Dad *love* Chris." Zoe beamed.

"That's good to know," Chris said, a smile lighting up his even, attractive features.

Zoe punched him in the arm. "Of course they do. What parent wouldn't?"

A faint stain of crimson hit his cheeks.

"Now you have to meet mine. Fair's fair."

Zoe bit her lip. "Yeah, okay."

"Good." Chris kissed the top of her hair.

"So what did you two get up to?" Zoe waggled her eyebrows, directing her attention to Lauren and Mitch.

"Zoe!" Now it was Lauren's turn to flush.

"Okay, okay." Zoe's expression grew serious. "I think it's great."

"Thanks. I was just saying to Mitch we should decorate the Christmas tree."

"Definitely!"

Lauren had a small artificial tree, since she'd read that a real tree could be toxic to cats.

She dragged it out of the closet, Mitch carrying it into the living room. She felt guilty that she and Zoe hadn't put it up earlier in the month, but they'd been busy with the café and play rehearsals.

The two guys set it up quickly, she, Zoe, and Annie sitting on the sofa and 'supervising'.

"I could get used to this." Zoe giggled.

"Me too," Lauren agreed, admiring Mitch's lean, muscular frame as he dealt with the tree.

After a second, Annie added, "Brrt!" *Yes!*

"Let's get the decorations." Zoe jumped up.

Lauren and Annie followed her to her bedroom. Lauren's closet wasn't big enough to house the tree and the baubles.

"So how was last night really?" Lauren asked as Zoe grabbed the cardboard box.

"I don't think anything fazes Chris," Zoe replied. "He was totally cool about meeting Mom and Dad. And Mom whispered to me when we left that he was a keeper."

"Good."

"How about you?" Zoe gave her a keen look. "Yeah, I can see that last night went well."

"It did," Lauren admitted. "It was amazing."

"You deserve it to be," Zoe told her.

"And you deserve a great guy like Chris." Lauren smiled at her.

They returned to the living room with the box.

"Brrt?" Annie jumped on top of the box, trying to lift one of the cardboard flaps with her paw.

"You can help us," Lauren told her.

"Yes, you can tell us where each decoration should go," Zoe added.

"Brrt!" *Good!*

They placed the large fabric balls on the bottom branches of the green artificial pine, then smaller decorations on the top branches.

"It looks great." Lauren stepped back and surveyed their work.

"It definitely does." Mitch wrapped his arm around her waist and held her close.

Annie wriggled under the lowest branch, turned onto her back, and batted a ball with her paw. The gold and cream decoration swung back and forth, tempting Annie to bat it again.

"It looks like the tree has Annie's seal of approval," Zoe declared.

"Brrt!"

***

On Monday, the new couch arrived.

"About time," Zoe said as the delivery truck pulled up in front of the cottage.

She and Zoe had already pushed the old sofa a little to the right, and moved the current coffee table to the left.

"I can't wait until the guys see the new sofa." Zoe grinned as she opened the front door. "I wonder if they'll like sitting on pink, or will it be too girly for them?"

"They mightn't mind as long as it's comfy," Lauren replied. She and Zoe hadn't done anything about ordering slip covers for the old sofa yet, deciding to wait until their new purchase arrived.

Once the delivery men had brought the sofa and coffee table in and plonked them into place, Lauren pulled off the plastic wrapping.

"It looks amazing." Zoe admired the pretty couch. It fit snugly next to the old blue sofa, and the pink and blue shades seemed to complement each other.

"This extra coffee table will come in handy." Lauren pushed the small oak table in front of the new furniture.

"Brrt!" Annie jumped onto the sofa and leaped from one seat to the other.

"I think Annie approves." Lauren laughed.

"So do I." Zoe sank down.

Lauren joined her, Annie sitting in her lap.

"Why don't we claim this new sofa, and the guys can sit in the old one?" Zoe's eyes sparkled with mischief.

"Why not?" Lauren teased.

"Brrt!" *Yes!*

***

On Tuesday, Lauren yawned as she unlocked the café at nine-thirty. Mitch and Chris had come over the previous night, and although Mitch hadn't slept over, they'd all stayed up late watching a spy drama – Annie, Lauren, and Mitch on the new sofa, and Zoe and Chris on the old one. They'd flipped for it.

Next time, it would be Zoe and Chris's turn to sit on the pink couch.

"Maybe we should have gone to bed earlier," Zoe admitted as she sat on a stool behind the counter, rubbing her eyes. "But that show was so good! I kept thinking it must be the guy who was the double agent, but it was actually the girl who was the triple agent!"

"I know," Lauren agreed.

"Brrt!" Annie called from her bed, before closing her eyes and nestling into the blankets.

Mrs. Wagner, wearing an emerald pantsuit, entered a few minutes later.

"Hello," she greeted the trio.

"Brrt?" Annie ambled toward her.

"Thank you, Annie." Mrs. Wagner followed the feline to a small table near the counter.

Zoe nudged Lauren. "It keeps bugging me about how we saw her at the furniture store."

"You mean how you saw her. I didn't."

"Because you were hiding," Zoe reminded her.

"We both were."

"Yeah," Zoe admitted. "Anyway, I'll go over there and take her order."

Zoe zipped to the table. Annie had returned to her basket, sensing Mrs. Wagner didn't want feline company.

Lauren followed, wondering if she would have to rein in Zoe. Her cousin could get a little carried away at times.

"I'll have a latte and one of Ed's Danishes," Mrs. Wagner told Zoe. She craned her head toward the glass case holding the tempting baked goods. "You do have his pastries today, don't you?"

"Yes." Lauren joined them. "Honeyed walnut, and apple Danish this morning."

"I do like his honeyed walnut. I'll have that."

"Coming right up," Lauren promised. She waited for Zoe to head back to the counter with her – in vain.

"Yes, Zoe?" Mrs. Wagner asked. "Was there something you wanted?"

Zoe shifted from one sneaker-clad foot to the other.

"We saw you," she burst out.

"Saw me? What does that mean?" Mrs. Wagner frowned.

"At the furniture store. In Sacramento."

"Oh." Mrs. Wagner's expression cleared, then became truculent. "So?"

"So, we were shopping for a new sofa."

186

There was a pause.

"That's nice," Mrs. Wagner finally said.

"Were you shopping for new furniture too?" Zoe asked after a beat.

"Zoe!" Now it was Lauren's turn to nudge her cousin.

"Why do you ask?" Mrs. Wagner stared at Zoe, as if daring her to blink first.

"Because – because—" for once Zoe seemed lost for words.

"We'll make your order right now." Lauren dragged Zoe toward the counter.

"She wouldn't answer my question." Zoe's face was a combination of shock and surprise.

"She didn't have to," Lauren told her as she poured coffee beans into the hopper.

"But …" Zoe seemed lost for words – again.

"It's none of our business what she was doing at the furniture store," Lauren told her.

"It is if she's a suspect!"

"Keep your voice down," Lauren said in a hushed tone. She flicked a glance toward Annie's basket but the feline seemed to be dozing.

Mrs. Wagner was checking her phone, not seeming to be aware of their conversation behind the counter.

"I know why she wouldn't tell me." Zoe took a deep breath. "She killed Jay, stole the money from his wallet, then went on a spending spree!"

"To buy new furniture?" Lauren whispered. She didn't feel comfortable discussing this while Mrs. Wagner was in the café with them.

"Yes!"

"Wouldn't she buy a new rose bush first, since Jay destroyed her rare one?"

"Maybe she already has. We'd better do some sleuthing after work today."

"What sort of sleuthing?" Lauren asked, a sinking feeling in her stomach.

"I'll tell you later." Zoe flicked a glance at Mrs. Wagner still looking at her phone.

"Okay."

Lauren brought the order over to Mrs. Wagner. "Let me know if there's anything else you'd like," she said.

"Thank you." Mrs. Wagner nodded.

Lauren headed back to the counter. Surely Zoe was mistaken about Mrs. Wagner? She couldn't imagine the woman killing anyone. But – she had seemed upset about Jay destroying her valuable rose bush, and she'd told them she hadn't been able to find a replacement.

A few more customers arrived, which kept the trio busy. When Mrs. Wagner paid her bill, Lauren took her cash.

"You should tell Zoe she shouldn't be so nosy," Mrs. Wagner told her. "Some people don't like it."

Was that a threat – or a warning? Lauren straightened her shoulders.

"I'll tell her," she replied evenly. Maybe Zoe was right – maybe Mrs. Wagner killed Jay.

She didn't have a chance to speak to Zoe until an hour later. She gave her cousin the run down.

"I knew it!" Zoe's brown eyes glinted with determination. "We are definitely checking out her place after work."

"Okay," Lauren agreed dubiously.

The rest of the day passed in a blur – apart from Mitch stopping by on his lunch break. Zoe took over, leaving her free to spend a few minutes with him at a rear table – Annie joining them as well.

They made arrangements for dinner that night – he'd come over to the cottage and cook.

"I'll buy some steak after my shift," he told her.

"Okay," she replied softly. Should she tell him what Zoe had planned for after work? She'd tell him at dinner, she promised herself. She and Zoe could hurry over to Mrs. Wagner's, see if she had a new rosebush, and then head back to the cottage. Mitch wasn't coming over until seven, which would give them plenty of time for their snooping.

"Brrt?" Annie asked, looking at Mitch inquiringly.

"I think she's asking if you're going to bring her some steak as well," she told him. "She likes it raw, cut up into little pieces."

"Sure," he replied, a hint of a smile on his lips.

"I can cut it up for her," Lauren offered.

"It's no problem, I'll do it," he said easily.

"Brrt." *Thank you.*

Mitch got a call and had to leave, dropping a swift kiss on Lauren's lips.

She watched him go, a smile on her face. Then noticed Zoe swamped at the counter.

"Back to work," she said to Annie.

"Brrt!"

CHAPTER 14

"Let's go!" Zoe urged Lauren and Annie out of the café. It was after five, and they'd finished cleaning the space.

"I don't think this is a great idea," Lauren warned, as they got into the car to drive the short distance. The sky was dark blue and the sun had set almost an hour ago.

"I think it's a perfect idea."

"We have to be back by seven," Lauren reminded her. "Mitch is coming over."

"And Chris." She grinned. "It looks like we'll be having dinner together."

"That will be fun." Lauren meant it.

"Brrt!" *Yes!*

"After dinner Chris and I can get out of your hair, and give you two lovebirds some alone time." Zoe waggled her eyebrows like a demented head elf.

"You don't have to do that," Lauren protested, although it would be nice.

"We can talk about it later," Zoe declared.

They arrived at Mrs. Wagner's house, situated a few blocks away. It was a small Victorian, like a lot of the houses in Gold Leaf Valley.

Lauren helped Annie out of the car, and held on to her harness. A cold breeze ruffled her hair, and she shivered.

"Luckily I brought a flashlight." Zoe waved it in the air, the bright yellow beam exposing Mrs. Wagner's front garden. "Now all we have to do is check out her plants and see if there's a new rose bush."

"How are we going to know if it's new?" Lauren stopped outside the gate. "We haven't visited her before."

Zoe paused as well.

"Huh. We could see if the tag looks recent," she finally suggested.

"If it has a tag," Lauren said.

"Brrt!"

Zoe led the way into the garden, the terracotta colored gate creaking a little as she pushed it open.

"I hope Mrs. Wagner doesn't hear us," Lauren said, thinking that just maybe this was *not* a good idea.

"She's probably watching TV. She'll never know we came."

The front garden was divided into two by a concrete garden path. On each side of the lawn were a row of bushes.

"We'll check this side first." Zoe flashed the light on a green bush. "Nope, I don't think that's a rose."

"Is that Jay and Kyle's house?" Lauren gestured to the dwelling next door. It looked a little run down in the gloom, and of the same era as Mrs. Wagner's. There was a large gap in the middle of the wooden fence dividing the properties – had Jay removed that section in order to plant hops, as Mrs. Wagner had informed them days ago?

"Brrt?" Annie sniffed the air.

"Can you smell smoke?" Zoe wrinkled her nose.

"Yes."

"We'd better check it out." Zoe charged next door, Lauren and Annie following.

They followed the scent of smoke to the backyard, walking along the driveway.

"Why did you have to be her favorite?" Kyle stood over a small bonfire in the twilight, sobbing. "It's not fair. I was the good one." A torn photo was half burned, flames licking the scrap that was left.

"I think we should go." Lauren tapped Zoe's arm. "We're intruding." She kept her voice low.

"Yeah," Zoe agreed. She swiveled around. "Come on."

"Who's there?" Kyle demanded.

"Um … it's me and Lauren," Zoe said in a bright voice. "And Annie. We've got the wrong house. Sorry."

"Yes, we were looking for Mrs. Wagner's house," Lauren added, taking a few steps away from the bonfire.

"She's next door." Kyle came toward them. "She'll probably tell you about how Jay destroyed her precious rose bush. And it's all true." Tear marks tracked down his cheeks. Lauren averted her gaze.

"Thanks. Sorry to disturb you." Zoe backed away.

"Come on, Annie." Lauren urged her down the driveway and toward Mrs. Wagner's house.

"You're dating the detective." Kyle followed them. "He won't tell me anything about the case."

"He hasn't told me anything either," Lauren replied. *At least not for the last few days.*

"Yeah." Zoe nodded. "Mitch is really by the book."

"What about the witness?" he persisted. "There's no way that old guy could have seen me." He froze, his mouth parting, as if he realized what he'd just said.

Lauren, Annie, and Zoe froze as well. Then they recovered.

Zoe dug her phone out of her jacket pocket.

"I'm calling the police."

"No! Don't do that!" He lunged for her phone. Zoe took a step back.

"Why did you do it?" Lauren asked, glancing down at Annie, who looked poised for action.

"I didn't do anything," he blustered. "You misheard me."

"Okay." Zoe nodded, taking another step back. Lauren and Annie copied her. "See you around."

"Yes." Lauren noticed her cousin clutched her phone to her side. "See you."

"Okay, I'll tell you. But only if you promise not to call the cops."

Lauren and Zoe looked at each other. Then Lauren looked down at Annie, who returned her gaze with wide green eyes, as if waiting for a signal from her.

"It was an accident," he said desperately, when they didn't respond. "I didn't mean to kill my brother."

"What happened?" Lauren asked, her heart beating so hard, she wondered if anyone else could hear it.

"I brought a knife from home to cut some of the rope that had been tangled up backstage. So when Jay and I went over to the theater that Monday to help clean up after the production, I was going to cut out the knot and coil up the rope."

"I don't think that happened," Zoe muttered.

"No." Kyle shook his head. "I got into an argument with Jay. See, he asked to

197

borrow some money from me and I said no. He's never been good with his finances and if I lent him some – again – it meant I would be short for the month. But he didn't seem to care – as usual. And then he said, "Don't worry bro, when I inherit I'll pay you back."

There was a pause.

"You're not going to inherit?" Lauren guessed delicately.

"No." Anger and distress flashed across his face. "I was – along with Jay – equally. And then Mom decided to change her will."

"I'm sorry," Lauren offered.

"Yeah," Zoe added.

"I was always the good brother, you know? Always looking out for Mom – and Jay. And what did it get me?" His tone was bitter. "A big fat nothing, that's what."

"Oh." Lauren took a tiny step back, Annie following. So did Zoe.

"Mom had a stroke which is why she ended up in assisted living. She just wasn't the same when she recovered afterwards. You might have noticed she was frail when she came to see the Christmas play."

"We did," Lauren admitted.

"My brother's always been a bit of a screw-up but somehow he made it work for him. 'Kyle, you've got to help Jay. He's not as smart as you. Kyle, do this for your brother because he'll make a mess of it otherwise." He mimicked a woman's voice. "I tried to help my brother as much as I could but sometimes I got sick of it. And there's Jay, lapping up all the attention from Mom, playing the helpless son. And now Mom decides he's so helpless that he should get all her money when she passes, because he can't provide for himself."

"Wow, that's unfair," Zoe said.

"Apparently, I'm smart enough and work hard enough, so I can forge ahead on my own, while Jay gets looked after – again. So when Jay made that crack about paying me back when he inherits Mom's estate, I lost it."

"That's totally understandable," Zoe told him.

"Yes, it is," Lauren said as she and Annie took another step back. So did Zoe.

"I had the knife in my hand because I was about to start cutting the knot. I don't know what happened next." He shook his head, as if bewildered he couldn't remember. "And then Jay was lying there in the dressing room, with blood coming out of his stomach." His voice broke.

"What did you do then?" Lauren asked softly.

"I got rid of the knife in the storm drain outside the back door. Washed my hands in the backstage bathroom, made sure there weren't any traces left – I used a ton of the soap that was there – and then went out to get burgers for us."

"Your alibi," Zoe breathed.

"Yeah. And it would have worked too, if that old guy hadn't spotted me – us – arriving at the theater. I didn't think anything of it at the time, since I didn't have any intention of killing Jay then. We were the only ones in the theater. Luckily that old guy wasn't there when I got rid of the knife."

"You mean Hans," Lauren informed him. "'The old guy.'"

"I guess." Kyle shrugged. "He was the only person around. I was wearing a scarf, so after, when I thought about it, I hoped it would muffle my face enough so I wouldn't be recognized. And Jay and I haven't lived here long, anyway – I've been busy with work and visiting Mom so I haven't had time to meet people."

"Is that why you helped out with the play?" Zoe asked.

"Brrt?" Annie added.

"Yeah. Mom thought it would be good for us." He laughed harshly. "I'm forty-three and still do what my mother tells me to." He shook his head. "Pathetic."

"Jay helped backstage as well," Lauren pointed out.

"Because he wanted to stay in Mom's good books," he replied. "He knew all he had to do was go running to Mom and ask for money and she'd usually say 'How much?' even though she'd tell him he needed to take better care of his finances. He had her wrapped around his little finger so he could get away with practically anything."

"That must have been annoying," Zoe observed.

"You have no idea." Kyle scowled. "I'm telling you, being good isn't everything it's cracked up to be."

"I'm sure the police will understand if you tell them everything," Lauren said, hoping she was correct.

"Yeah." Zoe brought her phone up from her hip. "I'll just call them now and you can explain to them what happened, just like you told us."

"No!" The expression on Kyle's face morphed into terror. "You can't tell them. And you can't tell Mom. Jay's death nearly destroyed her. If she finds out I killed him, it will finish her off."

"I am sorry," Lauren told him, "but we need to do the right thing and tell Mitch. Maybe he can help break the news gently to your mom."

"Good idea." Zoe nodded, pressing the buttons on her phone. "Let me just—"

"No!" Kyle lunged forward and knocked the phone out of Zoe's hand. "I won't let you!"

Zoe's eyes widened in outrage. "No one does that to my phone!"

She grabbed the top of a green leafy bush and pulled. A handful of spiky leaves came away. She flung them at Kyle.

"Let's go!" she ordered Lauren and Annie.

"Ow!" Kyle's hands flapped at his face. "You scratched me!"

Lauren and Annie raced down the driveway alongside her.

"What is going on?" Mrs. Wagner appeared on her porch, a disgruntled expression on her face. "What is all this commotion?"

"Help!" Lauren called, sprinting through the gate behind Annie, who led the trio toward the porch.

"Yeah, lock the door behind us!" Zoe instructed as she zoomed into the hallway. "He's the killer!"

The door slammed shut behind them, then the sound of a bolt.

"Would someone like to tell me what is going on?" Mrs. Wagner asked, her hands on her hips.

***

"This is good tea," Zoe praised, wrapping her fingers around the blue mug.

"Thank you." Mrs. Wagner nodded.

Lauren, Annie, and Zoe sat in Mrs. Wagner's living room. After they told her about their escape from the clutches of a killer – Zoe's version – they'd called the police. Who'd arrived quickly and apprehended Kyle as he loaded a suitcase into his car. Now, they were just waiting for Mitch.

"And this sofa is really comfy." Zoe relaxed into the red plaid cushions.

"Yes." Lauren sat beside her cousin, Annie at her feet. "Thank you for the tea," she added, taking a sip of the English Breakfast brew.

"It's the least I can do." Mrs. Wagner sank into a matching armchair. "I had no idea Kyle killed his brother." She shook her head. "To think I was 1 living next door to him all this time. You just don't know about people, do you?"

"You certainly don't," Lauren agreed.

"Brrt!"

"Is this lounge suite new?" Zoe asked. "Our couch arrived yesterday and we love it already."

"Yes." Mrs. Wagner hesitated. "You asked me yesterday about why I was at the furniture store. And I was too embarrassed to tell you. I bought this lounge suite." She waved a hand at the sofa they sat on. "My daughter gave me a gift certificate for Christmas – an early present, she called it – and said to spoil myself for a change." She briefly looked away. "I didn't like to admit – especially to you young girls – that I couldn't afford to buy my own furniture."

Zoe's eyes widened. "And we thought you wouldn't tell us because you were the killer!"

"Me?" Mrs. Wagner looked outraged for a second. Then she chuckled. "Oh Zoe, you do have an imagination."

"Sometimes," Zoe admitted.

"But if I were the killer, why would I be buying new furniture?" Mrs. Wagner asked curiously.

"Because I – we – thought you might have stolen money from Jay's wallet after you stabbed him. Because he destroyed your valuable rose," Zoe told her.

"I was very upset about my rose bush," Mrs. Wagner conceded, "but I don't think I would ever be upset enough to kill someone."

The doorbell rang. Lauren and Zoe looked at each other.

"It might be Mitch." Lauren spoke.

They followed Mrs. Wagner down the hall. After peering through the peephole, she admitted Mitch.

"Are you okay?" He looked at Lauren in concern.

"Yes," she answered truthfully.

"Thanks to Mrs. Wagner," Zoe added. "Brrt!"

After repeating the details to Mitch, they followed him out, after thanking Mrs. Wagner for her help.

"Anytime, girls," Mrs. Wagner said as she waved goodbye. And she seemed to mean it.

"Now we only have one mystery left to solve," Zoe announced as they headed home. "What will Santa give us for Christmas?"

CHAPTER 15

Christmas morning arrived. Mitch and Chris managed to get the day off, and the four of them had just finished making lattes in the kitchen, gathering in Lauren and Zoe's living room.

With Lauren's help, Annie had opened her Christmas stocking, stuffed full of catnip, food treats, and a feather wand. They'd taken turns to dangle the green feather in front of Annie.

Zoe gave Lauren a loom knitting kit, plus three balls of brightly striped wool.

"To help you with your knitting mojo," Zoe informed her with a grin. She also 'helped' Lauren by setting up the tool and weaving the wool around the plastic pegs, engrossed in the task. Lauren wondered if she would eventually get a turn.

The loom was forgotten when Lauren gave Zoe a present from her and Annie – pretty, dangly earrings featuring shining red stones that she knew her cousin had hankered for. Zoe put them on right away, seemingly delighted with them.

They remembered the guys – Lauren gave Mitch a new wallet, while Zoe presented Chris with a stainless-steel bracelet that was actually a clever multi-tool. "It's got screwdrivers, wrenches and even a lock pick!" Zoe enthused.

Mitch gave Lauren a bottle of perfume that she'd spritzed on herself a couple of months ago in a department store, the heady scent of rose and vanilla teasing her senses.

Zoe ripped open the red wrapping paper from Chris's gift – her eyes lighting up at the sight of a large pottery book.

"These pottery pieces are amazing," she breathed as she flipped through the glossy color photos. "Thank you." She looked like she wanted to kiss Chris right there and then – and keep on kissing him.

Mitch gave Annie a pink cushion covered in velvet.

"It's practically the same shade as our new sofa," Lauren complimented.

"I hope she likes it," Mitch replied.

"Brrt!" Annie pounced on it, then wriggled against it, her back brushing against the soft velvet as she closed her eyes. "Brrp."

Chris had offered Annie a catnip filled ball, which she'd played with earlier, chasing it around the room.

"Look at all these gifts!" Zoe's eyes now lit up as she gazed at the brightly wrapped presents still left under the Christmas tree.

"I thought we'd exchanged all our presents," Lauren replied.

"Me too." Zoe's gaze met Lauren's and they exchanged a quizzical look.

Maybe Mitch and Chris were responsible for the extra packages?

"Here's one for you, Annie." Lauren showed her a package wrapped in red paper and decorated with pictures of Santa Claus. She turned to Zoe. "Did you buy her this?"

"Nope." Zoe shook her head.

She gingerly unwrapped it for Annie, aware of Mitch's questioning gaze.

"Brrt!" Annie pounced on the big, fluffy toy mouse.

Jingle! Jingle!

She picked it up by the scruff of its neck.

Jingle! Jingle!

"Brrt!" Annie put it down on the carpet and stared at the furry gray toy for a second. Then she batted it with her paw.

Jingle! Jingle!

"Did you give it to her?" Lauren asked Mitch, although she was pretty sure the answer was no by the expression on his face.

"I wish I'd thought of it," he said ruefully.

"Me too," Chris added, sitting beside Zoe on the floor.

Zoe grabbed a purple and red wrapped gift that had *Zoe* written in large letters on a tag.

"I love opening presents," she declared, a big grin on her face. She tore off the paper with a crackle and gasped. "Pottery glazes! Oh, Lauren, how did you know I've been wanting these?"

"I didn't," Lauren confessed, crinkling her brow.

"Maybe it was from me," Chris joked.

"Was it?" Zoe looked like she was going to launch herself into his arms.

"Unfortunately not." He looked regretful.

She picked up the tag. "It just says Zoe on it." She glanced at Mitch.

"No. Sorry."

"Huh." Zoe spotted a large flat package near her. "Lauren, this has your name on it."

"It has?"

Zoe handed her the green and gold wrapped parcel. The tag just said *Lauren*.

She opened it slowly, glancing at Mitch, who shook his head.

"Ohh." A book with the most delicious cupcakes on the cover caught her attention. "I've been wanting this book for months! But it's so expensive. I was saving up for it."

"You never told me," Mitch murmured.

"Because I was going to buy it myself," Lauren replied softly.

They gazed at each other, smiling, until Zoe fake-coughed to get their attention.

"There are two more presents here." She pointed to a couple of packages with blue and cream wrapping.

Mitch reached under the tree and pulled them out.

"Mitch." He read the tag on one. "Chris." He handed it to his friend.

"Did you?" Chris asked Zoe, and then Mitch.

"No," Zoe replied. "I gave you yours earlier." She grinned.

"Just like I gave you yours." Chris smiled. The paper crackled as he tore it. "The latest thriller by my favorite author." He stared at the hardback. "I thought this was sold out – I couldn't find it anywhere, and it's not available as an eBook yet!"

Mitch unwrapped his small gift. There was a box inside. He carefully lifted the lid, his face breaking into a smile.

"How did you know?" He looked at Lauren.

"I didn't," she replied, bewildered.

"My watch broke yesterday," he told her. "I've had it for years. And this—" he lifted a silver watch out of the box "—looks exactly the same." He gently touched the glass face. "It has the same features, including a calendar and a compass. Everything I need."

Lauren's phone rang.

"Hello?" she answered, wondering who it could be.

Mrs. Wagner's voice sounded.

"Oh, Lauren, I must thank you and Zoe for my new rosebush. I have no idea how you managed to find that particular rare species, but it's just perfect. It's exactly the same as the one Jay destroyed."

"It wasn't me," Lauren told her, "but I'm glad someone gave it to you."

"Maybe it was your daughter," Zoe leaned over Lauren's shoulder and spoke into the phone.

"Oh, yes, of course," Mrs. Wagner replied. "That must be it. Have a wonderful day, girls."

"This has been a totally strange morning," Zoe stated. "Mysterious gifts under the tree, and someone gave Mrs. Wagner a replacement rose bush."

"You said it could be from her daughter," Lauren reminded her.

"Brrt!" Annie ran to the window and stretched up, resting her front paws on the narrow ledge. Her head tilted back as she looked out.

"What is it?" Lauren hurried over. The morning was gray and drizzly but she thought she caught a glimpse of a moving blur in the sky.

A jingle filled the air. But Annie was right next to her – *not* playing with her new toy mouse.

Was that a red sleigh near the clouds? Were there brown shapes in front of it?

"Reindeer!" Zoe breathed, rushing up beside her. She squinted. "I'm totally sure they're reindeer."

"Ho, ho, ho."

Lauren caught the faint sound, and her eyes widened. If Santa Claus was real, then the mysterious gifts under the tree made sense. Could today become even more magical?

It could.

Since they were having Christmas dinner together, they all helped prepare the food. Zoe and Chris had gone outside to pick herbs, leaving Lauren and Mitch alone in the kitchen. Annie played with her new toy mouse in the living room.

"I didn't get a chance to say this earlier today." Mitch took a deep breath. "I'm in love with you, Lauren Crenshaw."

Lauren's heart filled with joy.

"And I'm in love with you, Mitch Denman." She touched the gold L necklace he'd given her a while ago.

They smiled tenderly at each other, before Mitch cupped her face and kissed her.

A faint "*Ho, ho, ho,*" echoed in the background.

Yes, this Christmas Day was indeed magical.

THE END

I hope you enjoyed reading this mystery. Sign up to my newsletter at www.JintyJames.com and be among the first to discover when my next book is published! Stay tuned for book 10 in 2021!

TITLES BY JINTY JAMES

Purrs and Peril – A Norwegian Forest Cat Café Cozy Mystery – Book 1

Meow Means Murder – A Norwegian Forest Cat Café Cozy Mystery – Book 2

Whiskers and Warrants – A Norwegian Forest Cat Café Cozy Mystery – Book 3

Two Tailed Trouble – A Norwegian Forest Cat Café Cozy Mystery – Book 4

Paws and Punishment – A Norwegian Forest Cat Café Cozy Mystery – Book 5

Kitty Cats and Crime – A Norwegian Forest Cat Café Cozy Mystery – Book 6

Catnaps and Clues – A Norwegian Forest Cat Café Cozy Mystery – Book 7

Pedigrees and Poison – A Norwegian Forest Cat Café Cozy Mystery – Book 8

Maddie Goodwell Series (fun witch cozies)

Spells and Spiced Latte - A Coffee Witch Cozy Mystery - Maddie Goodwell 1 – Free!

Visions and Vanilla Cappuccino - A Coffee Witch Cozy Mystery - Maddie Goodwell 2

Magic and Mocha – A Coffee Witch Cozy Mystery – Maddie Goodwell 3

Enchantments and Espresso – A Coffee Witch Cozy Mystery – Maddie Goodwell 4

Familiars and French Roast - A Coffee Witch Cozy Mystery – Maddie Goodwell 5

Incantations and Iced Coffee – A Coffee Witch Cozy Mystery – Maddie Goodwell 6

Made in the USA
Monee, IL
07 June 2022